A MONSTER IN THE MAKING

AN ACCIDENTAL CREATION

CHRIS CSORDAS

A MONSTER IN THE MAKING
AN ACCIDENTAL CREATION

This is a work of fiction. All the characters, names, incidents, organizations, and dialogue in this novel are either the products of the author's imagination or are used fictitiously.

iUniverse books may be ordered through booksellers or by contacting:

iUniverse
1663 Liberty Drive
Bloomington, IN 47403
www.iuniverse.com
1-800-Authors (1-800-288-4677)

Because of the dynamic nature of the internet, any web addresses or links contained in this book may have changed since publication and may no longer be valid. The views expressed in this work are solely those of the author and do not necessarily reflect the views of the publisher, and the publisher hereby disclaims any responsibility for them.

Any people depicted in stock imagery provided by Getty Images are models, and such images are being used for illustrative purposes only. Certain stock imagery © Getty Images.

ISBN: 978-1-5320-5617-8 (sc)
ISBN: 978-1-5320-5618-5 (hc)
ISBN: 978-1-5320-5640-6 (e)

Library of Congress Control Number: 2018910218

Print information available on the last page.

iUniverse rev. date: 10/08/2018

1
CHAPTER

They say monsters are not born; they are created. Built and bred by the bitterest aspects of life, from the deepest, darkest holes in the human brain. A person can only be pushed so far before their mind goes from bending to breaking.

Conner was a small town in rural Ontario, Canada. It was the kind of small town where you couldn't even go to the grocery store without running into ten people you knew. That was a blessing for most. Some people who come from a small town develop a sense of security from knowing everyone. They slip into a comfort zone within which they believe nothing can go wrong and everyone is a friend.

That was true for most people in Conner, but unfortunately this wasn't the case for Ben. He was an eleven-year-old boy with dirty-blond hair and light blue eyes. He was overweight, but because he was taller than all the kids his age, it didn't look as obvious. All the other kids would refer to him as retard when they addressed him. His soft nature made it impossible for him to stick up for himself.

Despite the bullying, he was always nice and polite to everyone he met. He did have friends while growing up, but as they got older, they started becoming enemies. His last friend, Jason, who was a childhood friend, had always been there for him. Jason was a geeky kid. He had thick glasses, a mushroom cut, and a unibrow. He always wore the same blue jeans and a baggy rock band T-shirt. Once he became really interested in girls, he told Ben he couldn't be seen with him anymore. Jason jumped sides, as Ben would refer to it, when they hit grade seven and being cool and who one hung out with became more important than an actual friendship.

Ben's home life was not much better than his social life. His parents had severe addictions to crystal meth, cocaine, and any other drugs they could get their hands on. They seemed to care more about where their next hit was coming from than their son's next meal.

Ben's mother, Amy, was tall, blonde, and skinny. From a distance she looked normal—beautiful, even. She had a chiseled jaw structure with a pointy chin. Big dimples when she would smile. But once you got up close, you could tell by the sunken cheeks and the terrible acne (which she tried covering up with an enormous amount of makeup) that she did not take care of herself. One look, and you would automatically assume she was a drug addict.

Before she became addicted to drugs, she'd been a very beautiful girl. She was very smart in high school but also had a very hard upbringing. Her parents were killed in a car accident when she was ten, and she was forced to live in foster homes till she was old enough to move out. She was treated like a slave in the foster homes and wanted nothing more than to be free of the system. When she turned eighteen, she immediately moved in with her boyfriend, Matthew Willis. Matt was a few years older than her. She was attracted to him because of his ripped physique and because he was taller than her. For a lady her height, that was not easy to find. His black hair and five o'clock shadow reminded her of her dad, and regardless of all the signs, she felt safe and protected with him.

Despite Matt having only a grade-nine education and Amy's suspicion of his drug use behind her back when they'd first gotten together, she loved him anyway. And he already had his own place.

Within a couple of months, she was pregnant with Ben. Matt started becoming more open with his drug use, and before long he was smoking crack and doing lines right in front of her. One night, when she was about seven months pregnant, Matt convinced her to do some cocaine with him. He was a smooth talker, and she didn't know much about drugs. She took his word that a onetime use wouldn't be harmful and stayed up all night partying. Before long, she was as addicted to drugs as he was. When she went into labor, she had so much cocaine running through her system that the doctors didn't know whether the baby would survive the birthing process, let alone have no birth defects. Despite all that, it was a successful delivery, and the baby was healthy. Or so they thought.

Ben was taken from Amy and Matt until they did a rehabilitation program, which they both completed as directed. Three months after that, Ben was back in Amy's hands, and she vowed to stay sober for him and to never put him in harm's way again. She and Matt relapsed a few short months afterward and continued down that road with no end in sight. Both were eventually hospitalized. Amy was diagnosed with schizophrenia. Matt was diagnosed with bipolar and schizophrenia. They were released on the condition that they'd take their prescribed medication, and they got Ben back.

It wasn't long before the system lost track of them. They were always getting evicted for not paying rent or for repetitive complaints from neighbors. They eventually settled down in an old, run-down house in a small subdivision just outside of town with only a few neighbors. It was on a one-acre property, but the land was filled with the landlord's trash and old farm equipment. It was a two-bedroom, one-bathroom house with an unfinished basement that had a dirt floor. It looked as if it were straight out of an episode of *Hoarders*. Most of the windows were covered with old, dirty bedsheets and towels, which gave it a very dark and creepy feeling, along with the drug paraphernalia everywhere.

Ben hated that his parents made him sleep in the basement. He hated the mold creeping up the walls and support beams. He hated the musky smell that stuck to his clothes. He hated that he didn't have a dresser for any of his clothes and that he had to lay his stuff out on garbage bags. It was a big square room with three tiny little windows. Under the one window lay a dirty old mattress that looked as if it had been pulled out of a dumpster. The sleeping bag draped across it looked as if it had been used in World War I.

For a pillow, he had a ratty old T-shirt he'd stolen from his mother. All his belongings were either from the local shelter or pulled out of a trash bin. There were no outlets in the basement, so he had an extension cord running down the steps that plugged into an old TV and a night-light.

When his dad wanted to be funny for their friends, he would unplug the cord upstairs, knowing Ben couldn't sleep without his night-light. Ben didn't know what was worse, the pitch black, which he was deathly afraid of, or the fact that he could hear them laughing when they did it. It was cold, dark, and lonely, but ironically it was the only room in the house where Ben felt safest. Amy wanted to get sober and provide for her child. She wanted that more than anything else. But every time she would try, she would be brought right back down by Matt, who had no intention of getting off the drugs or letting Amy get off them either. This led to a toxic, abusive, and resentful relationship. In no way was it a healthy environment in which to raise a child.

It was late June, and summer break was right around the corner. That was always a welcoming time for Ben. For most kids, summer break meant playing outside and having fun with friends for two whole months. For Ben, it meant no bullies or asshole teachers for two months. That was good enough for him.

During the school year, it was as if Ben had a target painted on his back, and there was no washing it off. He was the epitome of a bullied, defenseless kid. He never wanted any trouble, but it always seemed to find him. He was degraded and picked on daily. It damaged him in a way that made him very insecure, and anytime he was confronted, he would turn around and not walk but run the other way.

He could take getting bullied by people; it was what he was used to. It was when his best friend, Jason, turned on him and started bullying him that it started to hurt. Jason was a friend he used to look up to, a friend who would help him deal with the bullying. Now the friend became the bully. And worst of all, for some reason the teachers would always turn a blind eye when they saw Ben getting picked on. They would look the other way, or at the very most they'd start walking in the direction of them, so the kids would stop and run away. But the kids were never punished. Ben had an altercation in the hallway one morning, and the teacher who broke it up told Ben that it was good for him to be bullied because it would make him stronger for when he grew up and had to live in the real world.

That was truly hard for Ben because not only did he not have any friends to confide in, but his parents were no better. He couldn't go home and talk to his mom or dad about how shitty his day was. He didn't have that option. He was completely alone, so instead of dealing with his problems, he learned to stuff them so far down that he couldn't even feel it anymore.

There was only one thing that got Ben out of bed every day and kept him from giving up. Like any other kid, he had a dream. That dream was what gave him the motivation to try to do well in life. He wanted to live the good life: nice car, fancy house. He would even dream about being able to buy his parents a house one day. He wanted to marry a beautiful girl and have beautiful kids. He was going to do all that by becoming a veterinarian—or, if all else failed, a pro wrestler. His passion was animals, and he loved them more than people. Mainly it was because they didn't bully or pick on him. They were nice to him because he was nice to them. There was no judgment involved at all, just love.

Like everyone else in the world, Ben had a happy place to visit when he was feeling down. It was a place where he could be who he wanted to be and do what he wanted to do with no consequences. But what happens when you lose that happy place, and the only thing you saw was darkness and the only feeling you had was anger? What happens when you are surrounded by nothing but hate and anger and negativity? Eventually everything a person thought would be just that. Everyone had a breaking point, and Ben was nearly at his. People can only take so much abuse before it is all they knew, so much pain before hatred of everyone became a security blanket worn as a suit of armor.

Ben eventually got to the point where he wished that he'd never been born at all, or that he would die already, because every day at school was a reminder of how alone and disliked he really was. And for no reason at all. It was torture in the most literal sense of the word.

Ben woke up and got ready for school and headed out the door. Just like every other day, he would judge the pace of the day by whether or not he got picked on while on the way to school. Today he did not. He thought it was going to be a good day. He got to the school bully-free and was walking down the hall to his classroom when all of a sudden he felt a hard blow to the small of his back that sent him crashing to the ground. His hands were full of books, and to avoid landing on his face, he had to throw his books to the ground and put his hands out to break his fall. His books and loose papers scattered across the hallway. He didn't even need to look up to see what happened; the giggling of the kids and the sound of their footsteps running away said it all. He landed on all fours and for about twenty seconds just stayed like that. Like a moment frozen in time, everything in the world stopped except for his anger. That anger filled him from his toes to his eyes. He could feel the hate start to overwhelm him. All he wanted was to beat the shit out of the kids who did this.

He was in front of his classroom door, and he turned his head to look into his classroom and saw his teacher smirking at him. Mr. Finch was in his early thirties, had short dark hair and thick dark eyebrows. He had glasses that he always wore hanging off his nose, and he always tried being friends with the cool kids in school. Upon meeting this guy, any adult would see right through him and instantly be able to tell that he was the kind of guy who sought revenge on the world for his own misfortune. He'd been a loser his whole life but didn't accept it and tried hard to be cool by hurting others. Now that he was older and had some power, Mr. Finch was trying to pull the same stuff. Sometimes he would even antagonize the bullying.

When Ben saw Mr. Finch smirk at him, it was worse than getting kicked to the ground by the other kids. He started getting visions in his head of his dad slamming him up against the wall and whispering to him, "I could crush your head if I wanted to." Then he'd get other visions of kids laughing at him and teasing him. It was as if he was reliving all those moments in his head, and he was about to burst from it.

He heard footsteps coming up from behind, and all he could do was hope it wasn't another bully. The footsteps got closer and closer, and with each footstep, a new bead of sweat developed on Ben's forehead. The footsteps stopped right beside him, and he saw a shadow standing next to him. He was about to get up and start swinging when all the sudden he was hit with this intoxicating smell that instantly calmed him. It smelled like strawberries and vanilla—a smell he'd never forget. The shadow bent over and started gathering all the loose papers. Ben looked up and saw the prettiest girl in school, Sam, helping him. When they met eyes, she smiled at him. He smiled back. It was like a little ray of sunshine in a very dark life.

"Those guys are jerks!" Sam said while she handed Ben the papers she'd gathered off the floor.

Ben was in disbelief at what was happening. The prettiest girl in school was helping him and talking to him, and all he could do was stare at her like an idiot as he slowly gathered the rest of his books and scattered papers. *She is so beautiful,* he thought. She had long, dirty blonde hair she always had in pigtails, the lightest blue eyes, and a very cute and friendly face. She had a yellow dress on with a white undershirt, and she always had a little purse she carried around with her. He was so nervous that when he went to say thanks, it came out as, "Yhank tou." She instantly laughed, but it was different this time. She wasn't laughing at him. He'd simply made her laugh over something they both found funny. They stood, and he corrected himself as she handed back his papers.

She responded with, "Wour yelcome." They both laughed again, and she headed off to class, which was two doors down. Right before she went into her classroom, she turned and smiled at Ben. He had never seen anything as beautiful as that smile. Any bit of anger he had in him was gone. He stood there for a second, absorbing this blissful state of mind he was in, until it was interrupted by Mr. Finch snapping at him. And just like that, he was brought back down to the cruel reality of his life.

"Ben, get in here!" Mr. Finch demanded.

Ben took a deep breath and headed into the classroom. He saw everyone was looking at him. Mr. Finch called him to the front of the class and began to scold him for being late, even though he'd seen what had happened.

All that rage rushed back. These flashes started coming back, but this time it was different. They weren't flashbacks of his life. They were visions of killing Mr. Finch. It was like the visions were depicting a movie in his head. He saw a pencil sitting on the desk beside him, and he envisioned picking up the pencil and stabbing Mr. Finch over and over again. The last vision was an image of Ben standing over Mr. Finch's body, the teacher's sweater vest fully soaked in blood. His glasses lay on the floor next to him. All the students huddled in the corner, fearing for their lives.

The vision stopped, and the fear he had of Mr. Finch wasn't there anymore. When Ben looked up from the ground, they were eye to eye. Ben could sense fear in Mr. Finch, and he developed a sense of power from it. He saw a weakness in his teacher he'd never seen before. He could tell Mr. Finch was intimidated, so the teacher demanded Ben sit down at his desk, adding, "And don't be late again."

Ben walked over to his desk. As he walked past the other kids, he could hear them whisper and laugh. Out of nowhere, he was hit in the side of the face by a big, wet spitball. The whole class erupted into laughter. He wiped it off and sat at his desk. After a few minutes, everyone was focused back on the teacher.

It was weird how something so devastating to one could mean so little to others. They really didn't have any idea of the affect it had on Ben, but all he could do was sit there, fight back the tears building up in his eyes, and stew in the anger of what had just happened. Usually he would sit there for the rest of the class, dwelling on getting made fun of. But this time it slowly faded, and after a few minutes, his anger was again replaced with the image of Sam's beautiful smile. He knew he didn't have a shot in hell with her, but he was grateful that she had been nice to him.

For the rest of the day, that was all he could think about. Every time he saw her in the hallway, she would shoot him a smile and a cute little wave. He would smile back and bashfully look down at his feet as his entire face lit up like a red light bulb. He felt as if he'd made a friend. He knew they would never be the kind of friends to hang out and go to the movies, but the simple fact that someone said hi to him during the day was enough.

Ben was in a great mood. The last school bell rang, and it was home time. He gathered up his stuff and walked out into the hallway. He would usually go left, walk out the side doors, and head home from there, but today he went right. He wanted to catch one more glimpse of Sam before he went home. She took the bus, so he had to walk to the other side of the school and go out the doors that all the other kids went out. There was a lot of socializing going on at the doors, and that meant he would be a target while walking through the crowds.

He headed down the hall and toward the buses. The closer he got, the louder it got. He stopped at the end of the hallway. It sounded like there was a sea of kids right around the corner. All he had to do was go around that corner and walk straight down the hall toward the front doors. He'd look up to find Sam, and then he'd look back down at the ground, walk right out the front door, and keep going no matter what.

He hesitated but pushed himself to go. The hallway was long, which gave him time to locate her before he got too close.

There she was, standing in a group of girls, talking and laughing with her friends. As he walked by the group, she was in mid conversation with her friends, and as she was talking, she looked over at Ben and shot him a tiny little smile. He smiled and looked back down at his feet.

That was exactly what he'd wanted. That was enough to make the rest of his night good, no matter what. He kept walking straight toward the front door. Just before he got to it, he looked up and locked eyes with the kid who'd kicked him in the back earlier that day, standing there as if he had been waiting for Ben. He had a big smirk on his face and was gesturing for Ben to come outside. Ben froze like a deer in headlights. Sam noticed this and watched from a distance. Ben stood there for a few seconds before he darted back down the hallway. She noticed a group of boys laughing and pointing at Ben as he went in the other direction.

Ben made it to the back door that he usually uses. Before opening it, he prepared himself for a beatdown. There was a good chance they'd run around the school to ambush Ben on the other side.

He walked out and looked around, making sure he still held the door open. The coast was clear. The moment he let that door close behind him, he was grabbed from the back. He couldn't see who it was because it happened so fast, but they grabbed his backpack, swung him around two or three times, and flung it into a tree. It knocked him out cold.

He woke up a few minutes later with a massive goose egg on his head. He also noticed he was soaked from his chest to his knees, and as he gathered himself and pulled himself to his feet, he saw he was covered in his own vomit and urine. He stood there for a few minutes in confusion, trying to wrap his head around what had just happened. He looked around, and all he saw was Mr. Finch getting into his car. Ben's anger focused on Mr. Finch. He wanted nothing more than to take that man's life into his hands and crush it for humiliating him in front of everyone.

Like everyone, Ben had those feelings of hate, those feelings of wanting to hurt someone. Punch him in the face. Kick him while he is down. Stuff most people thought about but wouldn't actually do. Ben's thoughts got more sadistic, more violent, more personal, and more probable of happening. The only thing Ben really feared was the idea of going to jail. From all his dad's horror stories of jail, that was the last place he wanted to end up.

For his entire walk home, all Ben could think about was the asshole who'd smashed him into a tree and then run away like a coward. And Mr. Finch. He hated Mr. Finch most of all. The more he thought about it, the angrier he got. As he walked home, any unlucky bug that had the misfortune of crossing his path would meet the bottom of his shoe, leaving a messy trail behind him. He did that all the way home until he was in front of his place. He spent ten minutes walking around, stomping on every bug he saw, and twisting his foot like he was stepping on a cigarette.

He noticed the neighbor lady watching. She was an older woman in her late seventies. She'd been widowed for years and didn't have any family that lived anywhere near her. All she had was her white Maltese dog. "Yippy little mutt," Ben muttered under his breath. She and the dog would spend hours out on the porch, watching everyone doing their thing.

Normally this didn't bother Ben. Any other day, he wouldn't have paid any attention to her. But today was different. Today it bothered him. He wanted nothing more than to take that dog away from her and watch her struggle to live without it.

When he noticed her watching him, he locked eyes with her and started stomping on the bugs even harder and letting out a yelp while he did it. He did this a few more times before he walked up to his front door while keeping his eyes locked on her like a hawk. Before he went inside, he stopped and stood there, staring at her.

She was trying to not pay any attention to him anymore, but she could feel his eyes looking and it was too much for her. She got scared and grabbed her dog and went inside. She immediately went to her living room window to see if he was still standing there. He was. He stood staring at the house with this expressionless look on his face. It was terrifying for her.

Ben turned and went inside. Upon entering, he saw his mom and his dad passed out on the living room floor, naked, with needles sticking out of both of their arms. Ben was good at adjusting to a situation. He'd learned to adapt to his surroundings and carry on. That was exactly what he did now. He walked past his parents like it was nothing, went into the kitchen, pulled out his school books, and started doing his homework. He started reading his book for English class but had the urge to look at his parents. He tried not to. He tried fighting that urge. He didn't want to see them like that. But he wanted to burn the image of what drugs did into his brain. He eventually gave in and looked over at them. They were both out cold. They were naked, exposed, and vulnerable.

Ben loved his mother, but this was becoming hard to handle.

He started getting these very disturbing visions in his head as he tried to focus on his book. These images seemed so real, as if they had already happened and were burned into his head as memories. The first image was of him standing over his parents with a knife. He felt as if he was taken to that moment in time and then slammed back into reality, but before he could even catch his breath, he was slammed back into another image. This one was worse. It was of him standing there, but this time his parents were all bloody, and he was holding a bloody kitchen knife.

The flashes went away after a few minutes, but what he saw was so real that he felt as if it had happened.

Just then, his mother woke up and came staggering into the kitchen. "Hey, baby. How was school?" she asked as she covered herself with a bedsheet.

Ben shrugged his shoulders and continued reading.

"Are you hungry? I think we have some fish sticks in the freezer, and I can make some homemade fries," Amy said as she rifled through the cupboard and pulled out a bag of potatoes.

Ben was hungry and got a bit excited for dinner. One of his favorite meals was fish and homemade fries.

Matt walked in a few moments later. He was in much worse shape and did not attempt to cover up at all. He dropped down in the chair across from Ben with a loud thud and the sound of skin slapping off the soft plastic of the chair. He could barely keep his head upright. Even in this state, where he could barely walk, he was still scary. He had a big scar on his cheek from where his dad had cut him with a knife one drunken rage—fueled night for leaving dirty dishes in the sink. One could tell by the salt-and-pepper hair and the blotchy skin that Matt was getting old, and what used to be shredded abs was now flab.

Amy started passing around the dinner plates. She set one in front of Ben, one where she sat, and one in front of Matt. The sound of Amy dropping the plate in front of Matt startled him. He snapped his head up, looked down at the plate, and swiped it off the table with his arm. It went crashing to the floor and broke into a million pieces. He slammed his forearms on the table and stared at Ben with a very angry, intimidating look. Amy started cleaning up the broken plate and ordered Matt to go back into the living room. This didn't break his concentration; he stared at Ben and wouldn't stop. Ben sat there, looking down at his empty plate, frozen like a statue, in hopes his dad would lose interest and leave him alone.

When Amy was done cleaning up, she walked over to Matt and started shoving him off the chair and into the other room. Matt fought back, grabbing Amy by the throat and pulling her in close. He didn't say anything; he simply threw her backward and stumbled into the other room. Amy watched till Matt sat back down, and then she fixed her and Ben dinner as if nothing had happened.

They ate, talked about school and homework, and laughed together. Ben almost felt like this was a real mother-son relationship, if it hadn't been for the fact that she was obviously still high. Even still, it was these rare moments they both cherished, knowing it wouldn't happen again for a long while.

Later that night, Ben was lying in bed. The lights were out, and the TV was off. It was about nine o'clock at night. He was just starting to dose off when a big bang came from upstairs, startling him awake. It was so loud that his body jolted, and he bounced off his bed and onto the dirt floor. He lay there for a second, not sure what the noise was and a little afraid to move. He heard his mother start screaming at his dad. Matt started yelling back, and that was when it got violent. It was nights like this Ben hated the most. Maybe it was because he was conditioned to expect the worst from always getting bullied at school, or because in Ben's eyes his father was an unpredictable monster.

When he heard his parents fight, he would instantly think of his worst fear and start believing it was going to happen. It was the idea of listening to his dad kill his mom during one of these fights and then coming for Ben in the basement.

On nights like this, all Ben could do was listen and hope for the best. He lay there completely still and silent in the dirt, just listening. He could hear the footsteps right above his head and could tell exactly where they were in the house. The stomps started getting closer to the basement door. All he could do was lie there completely terrified and hope that no one came downstairs.

There was a big thud followed by a couple of smaller bangs at the top of the steps just outside his door. The yelling and fighting stopped; it went completely silent. The only thing that went through his head was that his dad had just killed his mom, and he was next. He couldn't move. He lay there waiting to hear the creaking of the basement door open. It was the longest minutes of Ben's life. He expected the worst, but it never came. There was no more yelling, no more stomping. It was quiet. Dead quiet.

That was almost worse than when they were fighting because he had no idea what to think. The worst ran through his mind, and he couldn't take it anymore. He figured if his dad was going to get him, there was nothing he could do about it. He slowly pulled himself off the dirt floor, stood up, and walked to the bottom of the steps. He saw the door was open a crack, and for the next ten minutes he stood there as still as a statue, waiting to see if there was any movement or voices. There was nothing; it was completely silent. He lifted his right foot and quietly stepped down on the first step. He grabbed the railing and pulled himself up to the second step, then the third step, where he stood for a few more minutes listening. It was still silent. He started moving up the steps quietly till he could see into the kitchen through the crack of the door.

That was when he met the gaze of his father's eyes looking right back at him. But there was something very wrong. His father was lying on the floor on his stomach and coming from his head was a thick red stream of blood that slowly made its way to the stairs and dripped down on the first step. The only thing Ben could think of was that someone had broken in to rob their drugs, both his parents were dead, and it was a matter of time before they came for him. He was so stunned he couldn't move. He could do nothing more than just stare at his father. All of a sudden, the light coming through the crack of the door went dark, bringing an even darker and colder feeling over him. He slowly lifted his head to see what the dark shadow was when he met the eyes of his mother staring down at him through the crack. But it didn't look like his mother—it looked like a complete stranger who inhabited his mother's body.

She reached out and ripped open the door. Her eyes lit up with anger and evil. She had never looked at him like that before, and it scared the shit out of him.

He turned to run down the steps, but his mother grabbed him by the back of the shirt before he could move an inch. She dragged him into the kitchen and aggressively sat him down on a chair, not five feet away from his expired dad.

2
CHAPTER

Ben sat there in disbelief, never in a million years did he think his father would be the victim and it was clear to Ben from the slowly accumulating pool of blood leaking out of the back of Matt's head that the small thuds he'd heard at the end of the fight was Amy bouncing his head on the floor.

She leaned in the corner of the kitchen, staring at her son and her murdered husband, mumbling to herself. Then she ran over to his body and frantically started going through his pockets till she came across a little baggy. She pulled it out, went back into the corner of the kitchen, and proceeded to pack a bowl of crack to smoke it. She took a couple of tokes of the pipe and continued to stare at Ben, not blinking, moving, or saying anything. She slowly slid down the wall into a squat and didn't move for the next half hour.

Ben was so afraid at first, worried that if he made a move or even breathed loud, she would attack. That fear slowly turned into boredom and then hunger. He started to get restless and oddly was very accepting of the whole situation. The way he saw it, the body next to him wasn't his dad anymore. It was simply an empty shell. He didn't know exactly what had happened. All he knew was his dad was dead, he was pretty sure his mother killed him, and he was hungry. There was only one thing he could change. He contemplated it for a few minutes before deciding to stand up from the chair, walk to the fridge, and find something to eat. As he slowly stood up from his chair, Amy kept watching him with a curious look on her face. Ben stared back with the same look. When he fully planted his feet on the ground, he took a few more seconds before breaking eye contact with Amy, turning his back to her, and grabbing the butter from the fridge and the loaf of bread off the countertop. He buttered two pieces, walked over to Amy, and held his hand out with a piece of buttered bread. Amy took it out of his hands as the tears built up in her eyes. She didn't know what to say or what to do, and she was on the brink of a breakdown. She took a bite, and before she could chew it up and swallow it, she burst into tears.

Ben didn't know whether this was good or bad. He was still afraid of what she might do to him, but it only took one small gesture from Amy to make all that fear go away. She reached out and gently grabbed Ben by the hand. He pulled her to her feet and gave her a hug. She whispered, "I'm sorry you had to see this," in his ear before she pushed off and waited for a response. She had been crying for hours from before the fight, and she had tears, snot, and blood mixed all over her face.

Ben stood there, not sure what to say and not even really sure who this person was in front of him. They both stayed silent for a moment. That silence seemed to last a lifetime for Ben.

The silence was broken when Ben asked what they were going to do with the body. Since day one, his mother was all he had, and he knew that he had to protect her for her to protect him. It seemed like Amy was still trying to work stuff out in her head, but as soon as she heard Ben say the word *we*, she jumped all over it. Her face lit up like a Christmas tree, like a big weight had been lifted. "You're going to help me?"

"Of course I am, Mom. You're all I have."

Amy let out a deep breath of relief. She walked over to the sink, grabbed a cloth, and started wiping the mess from her face. When she was finished, she stood there, leaning with her hands on the sink's edge, contemplating what to do with the body.

"Okay, I have an idea." Amy said as she whipped around and looked at Ben. "We need to get him to the car. Are you all right to help me do this?"

Ben looked down at his dad and looked back up at his mom. "Can we cover his face up with something?"

Amy turned around and grabbed the dish towel that was hanging off the handle of the stove. She wrapped it around Matt's face and tucked it into his shirt so it wouldn't come off. It was a poor attempt to cover his face, but Ben didn't want to push the matter anymore. She positioned him at Matt's feet while she went around the top side of Matt.

"Okay," Amy said as she reached down and picked up the arms. "I need you to pick his feet up, and we are going to try to carry him to the garage and put him in the vehicle."

It took several attempts and some anger-fueled encouragement from Amy, but they were able to get the body to the garage. Now it was time to lift it into the trunk. That was more of a task than carrying him. They wrestled with Matt's body for half an hour, trying to get him into the trunk. They would manage to get him halfway up but then buckle under the weight, letting the body hit the concrete floor every time with a loud, cold thud.

They realized they weren't going to be able to do it and decided that trying to pull him through the back seat might be a much easier way to do it. The only thing was if they did that, there would be a good chance there would be blood stains left on the seats, so they would need to wrap him in something before putting him inside the car.

Amy grabbed a bunch of garbage bags and brought them out to the garage. They struggled with it but managed to get the bags around the body. After ten minutes, they were ready to pull him inside the car. They both lifted the top half of the body into the car, and then Amy ran around, grabbed the arms, and started pulling while Ben pushed at the feet. They got him in, and Amy decided it was a good idea to try to stuff him down on the floor and cover him with a blanket, just in case they were pulled over.

Amy told Ben to get into the car and added that she would be right back. He knew she was going back into the house to get high again. He jumped in the passenger seat and closed the door. As he sat there looking forward, he had an uncontrollable urge to look in the back seat. He'd always wanted to see a dead body. He flipped around in the seat and examined the body with his eyes at first. He pulled back the garbage bag and exposed some of Matt's chest. It was hairy, pale, and bony. He reached out and poked his chest, and when he pulled back his finger, he saw for a brief second an imprint in the skin. He reached out and poked it again. This time he noticed the skin was spongier than normal. He reached out and pinched it. It took a couple of seconds for the skin to flatten back out. Instead of being disgusting, he found it fascinating. He kept poking at the body a bit more till he accidentally moved some of the bag that was covering his face. Some of Matt's jaw and cheek showed. Ben stopped and stared for a minute. He reached out and pulled back the bag from Matt's face. Matt's eyes were bloodshot and starting to look milky, and he had a little bit of blood coming from his nose and ears. None of the evening had really sunk in till that moment. The moment Ben looked into his dad's eyes, he realized it was the last time.

He covered the face back up and turned back around in his seat. He wasn't really sure what to think anymore. He was fine with the body, but once he saw the face, everything changed. He tried to understand why a face made that big a difference. Was it any face? Or was it surreal because it was his dad's face, and he'd seen Matt as indestructible? He wasn't sure what to think, and he was to the point where he simply wanted to move past this night and put it behind him.

Just then, Amy walked around to the driver's side and got in. She didn't say a word, and her eyes looked like they were twice as open as usual. This scared Ben, so he sat there silent and went along for the ride.

They pulled out of the driveway and turned right onto the road. Everything he knew was to the left—the school, the grocery story, the whole town. They never went right out of the driveway; Ben didn't even know where that went. He sat back in his seat and watched.

After about ten minutes of uncomfortable silence, Amy broke it with a gasp. "Why did you even come upstairs? You never come up there when we are fighting."

Ben looked up at Amy. She was still looking forward while driving, and all he could notice was the light from the dash reflecting on her eyes, which seemed like they were bugging out of her head. Her face was still a bit swollen and bruised from the fight.

She looked over at him, expecting an answer. "Why?" she demanded.

Ben looked down at his lap and didn't say anything.

She reached out and shoved Ben into the door. "Why, god dammit?" She reached out again, but this time she slapped him on the side of the head. Ben took it and kept looking down at his lap, too afraid to say anything.

She reached out and swatted at him again. Then again and again. Ben put his hands up to protect himself, but she demanded he put his hands down. Afraid to do anything else, he put his hands at his side while Amy continued to smack him a few more times.

"You deserve this!" Amy said as she focused back on the road. "And you'd better not tell anyone about this, or you will be seeing your dad sooner rather than later." She took a few seconds to let that sink in a bit. "Who would even take care of you if I went to jail? Nobody, that's who. You would be on the streets and dead within a month."

Ben knew this and had no intention of trying to turn in his mother. The way he saw it, if one of them had to go, he was glad it was his father and not his mom. "I need you as bad as you need me, Mom! I would never get you in trouble."

"I'm glad to hear that, Ben."

They turned off onto a gravel road. Both sides of the road were thick with forest, and all the trees branches hung over the road and met in the middle, giving it a tunnel feeling while driving through it. They drove for another ten minutes before Amy started to let off the gas. She leaned over the steering wheel, trying to get a better look at where she was going. All of a sudden, she slammed on the breaks, sending Ben forward so hard that the strap of the seat belt dug into his chest a bit. She yanked on the steering wheel and almost put the car in the ditch on the one side of the road she meant to turn down. She just missed the ditch and kept going.

They drove for about half a mile before they came to a dead-end. Amy stopped the car, turned it off, and unlocked her seat belt. The sound of the seat belt sent shivers down Ben's spine. It meant it was time to get rid of a dead body. The moment would define Ben for the rest of his life, and that scared him but also excited him. He looked up at his mom for direction as to what to do. When he looked up at her, he saw her bring a pipe to her mouth and light the other end. The sound of crackling pipe and the clicking of a lighter was very familiar to him. He usually hated those sounds.

But this time was different. He didn't hate his mother this time. He didn't hate her for what she had done to his dad. He didn't hate her for beating him or for being an addict. For the first time, he saw a weakness in her, and it made him feel bad. It made him feel like he had to protect her and help her whenever she needed it. And that was exactly what he was going to do.

Amy put down the pipe and looked over at Ben. "You ready to do this?"

Ben didn't say anything. He simply shook his head, opened his door, and stepped out.

Ben stood staring at a beautiful lake, the full blue moon reflecting perfectly off the still water. A big wooden dock went at least twenty feet out into the lake. Amy walked around the front of the car and leaned up against it beside Ben. "It's beautiful, isn't it?"

Ben stared straight ahead, in awe at the scenery.

"This is where your dad took me on our first date." She laughed. "He was so nervous."

She looked over to Ben and brushed his hair back with her fingers. "He would have liked to be laid to rest here."

She stood up from the car, walked to the back door, and lifted the handle. "Ben, are you ready to do this?"

Ben looked at his mom. "Um-hm," was all he could spit out.

They dragged his body down to the water and onto the dock, which was more of a challenge than they thought it would be. She ripped the garbage bags off him, balled them up, and handed them to Ben. She laid Matt on the edge of the dock and stood up. She grabbed a crack pipe she had in her pocket, placed it beside him, and put a couple of empty beer cans next to him as well. She took a step back and with a proud look admired the scene she'd just created. Ben was blown away by this. He had no idea one could do such a thing.

Amy bent over, delicately rubbed Matt's face, said goodbye, and stood back up. "Do you have anything you want to say to your father before he goes?"

Ben didn't say anything. He stood gazing at the scene and the body and wondering whether she was going to get away with it.

"No?" Amy asked. Then she shoved his body into the water and pushed it toward the light current that went through the middle of the lake.

They both stood there in silence as they watched him float away into the dark water. It was a relief for the both of them, knowing he would never be there to hurt either one of them again.

After about ten minutes, the body was so far gone that they could not see it, so they turned around and headed back. As they slowly and silently made it back up to the car, not saying a word, they jumped inside and put that place in the rearview mirror. Amy made Ben promise he would never go back to that place, not even for a visit. She also told him to tell anyone who asked that Matt hadn't lived at home full-time for a long time; he came and went as he pleased. Ben agreed.

For most of the drive back home, it was pretty quiet. They tried soaking in what had happened in their own way. Eventually Amy broke the silence. "What are you thinking about right now?" she softly asked Ben.

Ben looked up at her. His face was only visible to her when they passed under the streetlights. "I was thinking it's good that Dad is dead. I was afraid of him, and now I don't have to be."

Amy looked back at the road and was stunned at how calm he was and how well he was taking all this. It was more than stunning—it was horrifying. He had no emotion at all, and he'd just helped bury his father. *There is something definitely wrong with that,* she thought.

They didn't talk much more for the rest of the drive until they pulled in the driveway. Amy put the car in park and turned off the engine. Ben went to open the door, but Amy stopped him.

"Ben, wait a second."

Ben stopped in his tracks and turned toward his mother.

"Do you have anything else to say about tonight? Are you worried about anything? Do you have any questions?"

Ben sat there for a minute thinking. "Why didn't he smell bad?"

Amy went silent for a moment and then said, "What?"

"I always thought that dead bodies smell bad. Why didn't he smell bad?"

"Honey, that doesn't usually happen till hours later. And that's not something you should be thinking about either."

"I know, but I kind of wanted to smell what a dead body smelled like."

"Why would you want to know something like that, Ben?"

"Just curious, I guess," Ben replied.

"Well, don't think like that. It's scary. I need you to be there for me, and I will be for you. We are a team and are in this together. You have my back, and I have yours. We can never speak of this night again, and you can never go back there. Do you understand me?"

"Yeah, I understand, Mom. Can we go in now? I want to go to bed."

They both got out of the car and went inside. Ben got cleaned up and asked if he could sleep in her bed tonight so he didn't have to be alone. Amy had no problems with this, except for the fact that she was going to be coming down off the drugs while she lay next to Ben.

For the rest of the night, she lay in bed and couldn't sleep. Not because she'd just killed her husband but because of what this might have done to Ben. She'd exposed him to a lot, and he had zero emotion. This was a very sobering feeling for Amy, and she decided she needed to change everything about their lives if Ben had any sort of a chance at a decent adulthood.

The next day, when Amy came out of her bedroom, she saw Ben sitting at the kitchen table, gathering all his papers and books for school and shoving them into his backpack.

"Where do you think you are going?" Amy snarled.

Ben rolled his eyes. "I have school today. It's a weekday, Mom."

Amy charged at Ben from the other side of the kitchen and swatted him upside the head. "Do not speak to me like that! You are staying home with me today whether you like it or not! Got it?"

Ben replied with, "Yes, Mom." Then he went to watch TV in the living room.

Amy made a pot of coffee and sat at the kitchen table. She sat there for the next two hours, smoking and drinking coffee. Ben wanted to approach her but thought that it might set her off. That was when he realized how afraid he was of his mother. That was when it all sank in. It hadn't really sunk in before this moment, and out of nowhere he felt a surge of emotion rush from the pit of his stomach all the way up. He was able to fight it, keep it in his throat that felt like a giant lump he was going to choke on, but he could only hold it in for so long. He could only stay strong for so long, and then he broke. It came pouring out of his mouth with loud, painful cries and screams. He started bawling his eyes out and couldn't control it. He wasn't crying because his dad was gone. He wasn't crying because he was afraid of his mom. He was completely overwhelmed with the sense of loss and abandonment. His worst fear was being left alone in this world with nobody.

Amy heard it from in the kitchen. She peeked around the corner and saw him break down and start crying. She went back behind the wall, and no matter how hard she tried, she could not wipe the smile off her face. To her, this was a good sign. He did feel something, and she hadn't completely killed him on the inside.

She walked into the living room and went to Ben, who was leaned over on the couch, still crying. "What's wrong, sweetie?"

"I don't want you to leave me too!"

Amy sat next to Ben and pulled him over to lean against her. "I'm never going to leave you, son. I love you."

Ben calmed down a bit. This was very comforting for him. He didn't have friends or any other family nearby. In his eyes, it was he and his mom against the world.

"I wanted you to stay home from school today because we need to talk about something."

"I know, Mom. Never talk about last night."

"Nope. Something else."

"What is it, Mom? Are you okay?" Ben looked up from Amy's shoulder with concern and tear-filled eyes.

"Yes. Well, no. But I will be," she said as she sat on the edge of the couch. "I am going to get sober, and that is going to be very rough for me over the next few days. I need you to do some stuff around here, which means you won't be going to school next week."

Ben knew what she meant about getting sober. He'd learned about drugs and alcohol abuse and the effects on the body through school, but mostly he got his knowledge from the internet in the libraries at school. He would hear his parents talk about drugs, and he would remember the names of them and then go to school to look them up on his lunch break. He knew what withdrawals were and how rough it was going to get. Despite all that, he was pumped about his mom getting sober, and he was willing to do anything to help make that happen.

"I will do whatever you need, Mom."

"Thanks, darling. I'm glad to hear that. I am already not feeling well. I'm going to call your school and tell them I am are really sick and need you to stay home with me. But I need you to go out and get some stuff for me. My end-of-the-month check was deposited this morning, so after breakfast I need you to take my bank card and go get the stuff on the list I give you. Okay? You will have to talk to the pharmacist."

"Yeah, I can do that."

"Thank you, Ben. Get yourself a treat while you are there," Amy said as she got up, kissed him on the forehead, and headed back to her room.

Ben made some toast with peanut butter, quickly ate, and then headed out the door. He was excited to do some adult stuff and help out his mom. Plus, he was pretty happy he didn't have to go to school for a few days. He got everything on the list, including the pills she needed that he had to get from the pharmacist. He was quite proud of himself and felt pretty good on the walk home.

Over the next few days, Ben stepped up to help out his mother. He saw sides of his mother he wished he'd never seen. She was violent and depressed and talked about killing herself. She had intense cravings, mostly at night when she would try to sleep.

He knew it would be over soon, so he tried staying away from her as much as possible, only talking to her when she needed something. After three days, the anger and aggression subsided, and she was a lot friendlier to be around. By day five, she was up and walking around, acting somewhat normal but being very forgetful and sometimes a bit hostile. But she was doing it. She was kicking that bad habit for her and her son, and she felt really good about it.

They started cleaning up the house a bit and decided to give it a complete clean. They moved Ben's room to the bedroom upstairs.

She went to get some of Ben's stuff from the basement and start moving it up, but before she reached out and grabbed the handle, she couldn't help but try to remember the last time she was in the basement. She couldn't remember the last time she'd been in the basement, and she barely remembered what it looked like. She grew very anxious, thinking about what she had her son sleeping in for all these years. It gave her a sick feeling in the pit of her stomach, but she headed down the steps anyway.

Most people living the same lifestyle as her tend to forget about the simple fundamentals of being a human being: love, respect, decency, truth. All these seemed to evaporate when addiction came into play. She couldn't turn away anymore. She had to see. While walking down the steps, she could feel the air getting colder and creepier with each step. The first thing she saw was a dirty, old mattress that was Ben's bed. Then she saw all his clothes laid out on bags. She was horrified. She turned around, ran up the steps, and headed to Ben, who was sitting on the couch and picking through a bowl of dry cereal. She fell to her knees beside him, pulled him to her, and started crying and apologizing for how she had treated him. Ben didn't know any better and was a bit confused. Even though Amy was brought up in foster care, she had still been taught the basic necessities of life. She had deprived Ben of almost all of them.

It was time for a change, and in a big way. For the next couple of hours, they sat in the living room deciding what was best for them and how they were going to fix their situation. She told him she was going to get a job, and he needed to be able to take care of himself when she was at work. And he should behave. She explained to him that the only way this would work was if they worked together and helped out each other. Ben agreed wholeheartedly and told his mom he would do anything she needed to help.

A few days later, Ben woke up in his new bedroom, happy for once. He walked into the kitchen and saw his mom in nice clothes, with her hair done up. She was standing by the table. "What do you think?" she said with a big smile.

Ben didn't really know what to think, so he stood there staring at her, trying to take in this new image of his mother. He had never seen her dressed like this before. He had never seen her wear something that didn't have a rip or a stain on it.

"I have a job interview!" she happily said. "It's in a half hour. What do you think?"

Ben gave her a big smile and hugged her. "You'll definitely get it, Mom."

"Aw, thanks, sweetie. Okay, I have to get going. I don't want to be late. I don't think I will be long, so I will see you soon." She ran out the door.

Ben couldn't help but feel excited for her. He thought that if she got a job, maybe there was a chance they could get a TV or even a video game player—it didn't matter which one. He started thinking about how cool it would be if he started getting Christmas presents or birthday presents. He imagined what he could ask for. There were so many things he wanted, but what he wanted most of all was his own bike. And not just any bike, but the coolest bike! It would be black with a fire red seat. It would have shocks on it just like ones he saw at school. It would have different gears so he could go fast or climb steep hills. He would have a fire red helmet to go with it. He started pretending he was riding a bike around the house, and he felt like a happy kid again, having fun and burning energy. He was having so much fun pretending to ride his bike that he took it outside so he would have more room to run around. He kicked open the front door as if he'd wheelied through it, and he did a sweet jump off the front steps. He landed and quickly banked to the right, hitting a little dirt hill to catch some air. After banking back to the left, he took it out to the sidewalk and started playing out there. A few minutes went by with Ben having the most fun he'd had in a while.

Then he saw Jason standing down the street a bit, laughing and pointing with his other friends. Ben got uncomfortable and immediately stopped pretending. Jason and his friends walked past, laughing and making fun of him.

"Haha, you loser. My dad said your mom's a crack whore. She'll never be able to get you a bike. Idiot."

This took all the fun out of Ben's mood, and he went back inside. He was angry at Jason, but he was angrier at himself for not doing anything about it and letting Jason push him around. He had to do something. He couldn't keep letting this happen.

About a half hour later, his mother came running in the door. "I got the job, Ben! I got the job!" She ran over to him, sat on the couch, and gave him a big hug and kiss. "I start tomorrow. Things are going to start changing around here, sweetie. I promise. No more going to the shelter for food. No more stealing water from the neighbor. We are going to get the heat and water back on. We might even get a TV and cable. How does that sound?" She had such happiness in her voice.

Amy's excitement helped Ben forget the bad mood he was in, and he started getting excited. Everything was changing for the better, and maybe he could find the confidence to stand up for himself to Jason. Then everything would be good. School would be out for the summer soon, and he wouldn't have to worry about it for a few months. He planned to use this summer to get stronger and more confident for the next school year so that he could stick up for himself to all these bullies.

Over the next couple of weeks, everything seemed to be getting better for the two of them. They both seemed happier. Amy loved her new job, and ever since Ben's dad had gone missing, the kids had left him alone at school out of pity. Amy got the utilities turned back on. They had food in the fridge for the first time in a long time. They had cable and TV. Things couldn't have been any better. Until one night when they were watching TV together, there was a loud firm knock on the door. Amy, not expecting company, curiously and hesitantly got up and walked toward the door. They usually didn't get unexpected drop-ins, especially at night, so this left her skeptical and cautious now that it was just her and Ben. She looked through the curtain and saw two men standing there. One of the men had a police badge on his breast pocket. She thought it was over. She thought she was going to jail and opened the door expecting the worst.

"Good evening, ma'am. I am Detective Flex, and this is Detective Coal. Was this the residence of Mr. Matthew Willis?"

3
CHAPTER

The man on the right was an older black man in his early fifties. He was wearing a blue pin-striped suit and a red power tie. He had a big belly and stood about six feet tall and was completely bald. He wore glasses that rested on the tip of his nose and was looking in a little notepad he had. The detective on the left was a young white man in his early thirties who wore a white buttoned-up shirt and a blue tie with black dress pants. He had on a black leather jacket and dark sunglasses, and his short blond hair was cut like he was in the military. He had a subtle arrogance to him like he knew everything.

"Yes, it was, sir." She turned to Ben and told him to get cleaned up and changed for bed.

While standing at the door, she pulled it into her as if to keep them from looking in and keep Ben from hearing anything they were saying.

"Was, ma'am?" Detective Flex said as he looked up and pushed his glasses back up.

"Yeah. He left a few weeks ago. I haven't heard from him since. Where is he?" she asked with some panic and concern in her voice. She had a way of playing the part and being extremely manipulative, and when she wanted to show concern on her face, she showed it with so much passion that one wouldn't second-guess what she's saying.

"Well, ma'am, I've been doing this job a long time, and I have learned that beating around the bush is the worst thing to do. I am going to be straight up with you if that's okay."

"Um, yeah. I think so. Like a Band-Aid, right?" she said with a nervous laugh.

"Right. Well, we found Mr. Willis. It was a few days ago and about two kilometers down the river. We would have come sooner, but he was so badly decomposed that we had to wait till the dental records came in to identify him. The coroner said judging by the condition we found him in, he had been dead for weeks."

"So, what? He fell in the water and drowned?" she asked.

"We are still doing an investigation, but when someone has been in the water that long, it's nearly impossible to pinpoint what exactly the events were that lead to his death.

We will continue with the investigation and keep you posted. We might come by again with some more questions."

"Of course. Whatever you need, Detectives."

"Thanks. Have a good rest of the evening, and we are sorry for your loss," Flex said, and then they walked back to the car.

Just then, Ben walked up and pulled at her shirt. "Movie time, Mom."

They sat down and got comfortable on the couch. Ben made a bowl of popcorn and set it on his lap. When the movie started playing, she found it hard to focus and couldn't stop thinking about the worst-case scenario if she were caught. Now that she was doing good and keeping clean, she didn't want to jeopardize it. She needed to be there for her son more now than ever, especially after what she had put him through. She spent the rest of the night thinking about it and found herself staring at the ceiling all night.

It was 7:00 a.m. when her alarm went off, and Amy felt like she hadn't gotten a wink of sleep. She got out of bed and went to the kitchen to make some coffee, and she saw Ben was already up and watching cartoons. Seeing that put a big smile on her face and made her feel good that she was able to finally provide Ben with the small stuff.

Life was becoming normal, and she wasn't about to let that change. She had to get it out of her head that she was going to be caught for her actions. After contemplating it in her head all night, she came to the realization that there was no way she could be blamed. She'd made it look like an accidental drowning.

A week went by, and Amy hadn't heard anything back from the detectives, so she decided to move on with her life and finally put it all behind her. Her life was for Ben now, and that was all that mattered. She was worried she'd messed him up so badly that she wanted to focus all her attention on making sure he turned out to be a good man.

Life seemed to be going well—until one night she came home from work, and the front window of the living room was smashed. There was glass everywhere. Ben was sitting on the couch watching TV.

"Oh my god. Ben, what happened?" Amy asked as she ran over to him. She started going over his body looking for any cuts or gashes he was trying to hide. Clearly, he had something to do with the broken window, or he wouldn't be relaxing on the couch watching TV. "Ben, what happened?" This time she was more demanding and angry.

"I don't know, Mom." Ben was still mostly focused on the TV.

This made Amy angrier. She was on medication for her schizophrenia, but there was only so much she could take before she got so angry that the medication didn't work. She was about at that point and could feel herself slipping into a dark place. She hoped that he would become intimidated and admit to what he'd done. This window was going to be very expensive and was going to cost her money she did not have. But then she felt herself completely slip away, and like a switch going off in her head, she became the other person. She grabbed Ben from the couch and slammed him on the ground.

The look on Ben's face was shock and fear because his mother hadn't done this in a while. But that shock and fear quickly turned to anger, and Ben lashed out and took a swing at her. This enraged Amy and made her even more violent toward Ben. She picked him up off the ground and slammed him back down, temporarily paralyzing him with fear as he struggled to catch his breath. He stared blankly into his mother's eyes and gasped for air.

Amy snapped out of it and scooped him up in her arms, apologizing and crying. Ben was scared, but at the same time he knew he'd done something wrong and was completely accepting of the punishment he just received. He was raised with the idea that if he did something bad, he would be hurt for it. His parents could never resolve conflict by talking, only with aggression and abuse toward each other.

That was all that Ben had seen while growing up. He didn't know any better way and thought it was just the way one did things. It was part of life.

"Why did you break the window, though, Ben? And why are you lying to me about it?" Ben stared at her with a blank look and didn't say anything. This angered Amy even more. "Why, Ben? Answer me!" she said as her grip tightened around his arms. With each word, she gave him a shake as she got a little more aggressive. Then she started shaking him so hard that his head snapped back and made a cracking sound. Ben instantly started crying. Amy was frustrated and angry, and she left him and walked into the kitchen, where she stood at the sink looking out of the small window that looked into the backyard. She stood there for about twenty minutes, not speaking or moving. In her mind, she was going over what it felt like to be high and not care. She missed the fact that she didn't give a shit about anything when she was high. She simply got high, and all her problems melted away. As she stood there, it was as if she kept slipping in and out of reality.

All of a sudden, a loud *bang, bang, bang* on the front door snapped her out of it. It took her a few seconds to find her bearings and collect her thoughts. By that time, Ben had stopped crying and was happily sitting on the couch and watching TV again. Another *bang, bang, bang.* She ran to the door, looked through the peephole, and saw those two detectives staring back at her. She panicked and yelled, "Just a second."

She quickly fixed her hair, straightened her clothes, took a deep breath, and put on her best fake smile. Then she swung open the door. "Good evening, Detectives. How can I help you?"

Detective Flex stared at the broken window with a puzzled look. "What happened to your window, ma'am?"

"Oh, nothing. Ben was tossing a ball around inside today, and the ball ended up going through the window. No big deal," she said, still smiling.

Detective Flex quickly shrugged it off and cut straight to the point. "We have some news on your husband. Do you mind if we come in?"

"Yes, absolutely. Come in."

She led them to the kitchen and offered them coffee, which they both declined. As the detectives sat down at the table, she went into the living room and told Ben to go into her bedroom to watch TV. She came back into the kitchen and sat across the table from the two men. "Sorry. I just don't want him to hear anything, and it's a pretty small living space." She laughed awkwardly.

"No, that's completely understandable. We had a call this morning out at this small lake in the country. There were some people going down there to camp, and when they headed down to the lake for a swim, they noticed a couple of blood spots on the docks. A bunch of empty beer cans and some drug paraphernalia rested nearby. We took some blood samples and found that it belonged to your husband, which would make sense given that we found him down the river that connects to the lake. In either case, we don't have any evidence or anything to indicate foul play to further this investigation and it had been ruled as an accidental drowning after a night of getting high and drinking. I just wanted to give you the courtesy of coming over instead of calling to tell you it's a closed case."

"I appreciate that, Detective," she said softly.

The detectives got up to leave, but before they did, Flex turned and said something unsettling to Amy. "One thing that didn't make sense, though. There were several blows to the back of Mr. Willis's head, as if it had been bounced off something a bunch of times. Now, I asked around, and the river he floated down is not a rocky river at all. Was he in a fight any time in the last week or so that you know of?" Amy shook her head no. "Ok. Even if you were not together as a couple at the time of his death, you are still legally responsible for the burial. We will have the documents ready to show the insurance company it was not a suicide so that you can collect his life insurance."

"Okay, thank you, Detective," she said, puzzled at the idea of Matt having life insurance. She'd had no idea.

The detectives got back into their car. Before taking off, Flex looked back up at the house and saw Ben standing off to the side of the broken window, staring at them. "There is something weird about that kid. I felt it the first time I met him," he said while still watching Ben peer out the window at them.

Coal didn't care much and was looking down at his phone, answering a text. "Yeah, they are a pretty fucked-up family, if you ask me. The kid's probably the one who killed the old man. The mom freaked and dumped the body to protect him," he said half seriously.

It was enough to intrigue Flex. "Maybe, Coal. Maybe," he said as he put the car in drive and pulled away.

The next morning, Amy woke up to her alarm at 7:00 a.m. As always, Ben was sitting on the couch, watching cartoons. She made a pot of coffee and started getting ready for work. After she sat down to drink her coffee, she called around to some glass installation companies and found one that gave her a good estimate. Ben was home all day and could wait for them to come.

Later that evening, when Amy got home from work, she saw the glass was broken again, and Ben was sitting there on the couch, watching TV.

"Ben!" she shouted, startling him. "Why isn't the glass fixed?"

Ben sat there silently as his mom stormed over to him. He anticipated the blows he was about to receive, but they never came. All she did was crouch down beside him and hug him.

"What's wrong, Ben? I know the glass guys came today to fix it. They called me when they were done. Why did you break it again?"

Ben simply hugged her back.

She realized that he was lashing out and probably depressed, sitting at home all day by himself. She thought it might be a good idea to hire a babysitter. Not only would he be supervised, but he could learn some social skills.

A few days later, Amy was at work and mentioned to her friend Marge that she needed a babysitter. She expressed how hard it was to find someone who wanted to give up a day watching a kid. One of the other waitresses overheard Amy telling Marge this and quickly intervened, jumping at the opportunity to get her teenage daughter out of the house.

"Hey, Amy. My daughter is looking for something like that," Kim said as she cleaned a table.

"Really?" Amy said with a lot of excitement.

"Well, I guess *I'm* looking for something for her," Kim said, laughing. "Her name is April, and she is seventeen. All she does is sit at home all day, and I'm sick of it."

Amy got excited and started asking questions, but Kim cut her off. "Whenever you want her to start, just say the word. It's not like she has plans. I wouldn't care if she did!" she said as she chuckled.

"I don't have to work tomorrow, so why don't you send her over to my place at ten o'clock to meet Ben?" Amy suggested with a big smile on her face.

"Works for me," Kim said as she cleared the last plate on the table and headed to the back.

Later that night, when Amy got home, she was making dinner in the kitchen while Ben sat on the couch, watching TV. She was worried about how he would take the news of having a babysitter, but she had no choice after two smashed windows.

"Come eat, sweetie," Amy said from the kitchen.

Ben walked in and sat down at the table. She noticed he was in a good mood and laughing a lot at the TV. She thought it was the perfect time to tell him.

"Sweetie, how would you feel about making a new friend?"

Ben perked up, as if he was excited about the idea of making a new friend. But he was quickly brought back down by the fact that every friend left him. "What are you talking about?"

"Her name is April. I work with her mother, Kim. Kim said all April does is hang out at home, so I mentioned she could come hang out with you instead. April is going to come by tomorrow. What do you think about that?"

Ben shrugged his shoulders as if to try to not show too much excitement, but deep down he was quite happy about making a new friend.

Amy was relieved that Ben didn't get angry or start a fight. He was oddly accepting of everything, which was unlike him. She thought maybe he was actually excited about meeting a friend. The more she thought about it, the more she realized she didn't know her son at all. Because of work, she hadn't been able to get to know him over the summer like she'd wanted. She started feeling guilty, and she had to get up from the table before she started crying. She walked over to the sink and pretended to do the dishes as she fought to stay strong and not break down. Once she started thinking about one bad thing, all the other bad memories came rushing to the surface. It was a surge of negative thoughts. She wouldn't let it show in front of Ben, though. She couldn't break down in front of him—she refused to. That was why she didn't leave the room. She simply toughed it out.

When she finally cooled off and calmed down, she turned to Ben, who was still at the table eating. "Ben, you know you cannot talk to anyone about what happened, right?"

"Of course, Mom. I know better than that," Ben replied.

Amy rolled her eyes and smiled as she gained the confidence she sought at his sarcastic response.

Ben finished dinner and picked out a movie while Amy cleaned up dinner.

"What movie did you pick tonight?" Amy said as she took a seat on the couch beside Ben.

"You'll have to wait and see, Mom." Ben got up, turned off the lights, and grabbed the blanket that was on the armrest of the couch. He curled up beside Amy and covered them both with the blanket. Before the opening credits, Amy was out cold. Ben didn't mind at all. When she fell asleep on the couch, it meant he could get away with staying up later then was normally allowed.

He would usually pick two movies and have the one set aside. When the first movie was over, he would wiggle himself free from beside his mom without waking her up, put in the other movie, and get back to the same position, curled up next to her. The times she woke up, he would pretend he had fallen asleep too. Amy caught on pretty quickly when she saw the opening credits for a new movie on the TV, but usually she didn't care. She would simply go back to sleep or watch the movie with him. The times she didn't wake up, Ben still wouldn't make it past the first half hour of the second movie. He would be fast asleep along with his mom, and it wasn't till they were both woken up by the end credit music that they retired to their rooms for the night.

The next morning, Ben woke up to the smell of eggs, bacon, and his favorite, french toast. He loved french toast and would eat it for breakfast, lunch, and dinner. He came running out of his room and was instantly taken aback when he saw two strangers sitting at the kitchen table with his mom. One lady was clearly the mother. She was tall and beautiful with long dark hair and dark eyes. She was always smoking and drinking coffee, and she always gossiped about people. She didn't have the best upbringing, so she always searched for flaws in other people. It was not because she wanted to feel better than them but because it felt good knowing there were other people in the world just as messed up as her.

She'd been raped and beaten as a child by her grandfather, and because they were a poor family, there was nothing anyone did. No one would have listened to her if she had said anything. She had never told anyone about it before. It was a big, dark, energy-sucking secret she had had to bear her entire life.

To the left of her was this beautiful young girl who couldn't be much older than Ben. When he saw her, he instantly got insecure and nervous. She was also tall with long dark hair, but she had thick dark eyebrows. Ben couldn't take his eyes off her. Both of her wrists had several rubber wrist bands and bracelets. There was glitter rubbed all over her neck and chest that made her sparkle every time she moved. Her white tank top, pink bra, and extremely short shorts resulted in the most skin Ben had ever seen on a girl that wasn't his mother.

"Good morning, sweetie," Amy said while fixing Ben a plate.

Despite the timid feeling, Ben's hunger pangs were worse. He slowly walked over to the table, and his mother set down his plate for him—right beside the pretty young lady.

With all three of them looking at him, Amy asked politely, "Aren't you going to say hi, Ben?"

Ben looked up from his plate and muttered, "Hello," barely loud enough for them to know he'd said anything at all. The girls looked at him and snickered, but in a "You're cute" way. They continued with the conversation they'd been having before Ben had come into the room. While they talked, it gave Ben some time to observe their behavior and try to get used to their presence. He figured this was the girl his mom had told him about last night at dinner, the one who was going to come hang out and be his friend. To his surprise, he was blown away by how pretty she was. He instantly fell in love with her, and after a bit, he couldn't stop staring at her. Every time April looked over at him, he would quickly look away. Then he'd look back up at her when she stopped paying attention to him. She found it cute and kind of flattering that he was so attracted to her; she didn't find it creepy at all. Eventually she started messing with him, and when she would look away, she would quickly look back at him to catch him. They both started laughing, which broke the ice and gave Ben the courage and comfort to ask her if she wanted to check out some of his DVDs. She said yes.

As they went through the DVDs, for the first time, Amy was able to sit back and watch Ben have fun with a friend, seeing the happiness in his eyes. She could tell he was a little embarrassed at times when he would start to fumble his words really bad, but April would place her hand on his arm, wait, and listen. Then he would eventually calm down and say exactly what he wanted. Amy hadn't seen that side of him, and he seemed like a completely different boy. She felt a sense of relief and thought maybe he would get away with having a good, normal life after all the shit he'd been through. For the rest of the morning, Amy sat at the kitchen table, half listening to Kim gossip about the other girls at work and half watching Ben interacting with April. She could sit there all day and watch Ben having fun.

A few hours went by, and Kim and April had to go. Ben was a little disappointed they had to leave, but he knew she would be back tomorrow. As they were about to walk out the front door, April turned to Ben and rubbed her hand on his head. "I'll see you tomorrow, little buddy." Ben smiled and went red in the face.

School was starting up in a couple of weeks, so when April and Kim left, Amy got Ben ready to go sign up for school, and they headed out the door. Amy was going to take Ben back-to-school clothes shopping as well. She couldn't remember the last time she had been able to do that, and she felt good about it. They signed up for school, and on their walk home, they stopped at the mall to pick up a couple of things. She didn't want to get all the school items quite yet, but she felt the need to treat her son with some new cool shoes and a shirt.

Upon entering the shoe store, Ben instantly noticed a cool pair of shoes on the wall that he really liked. They were all red shoes that had flames going from the toe to the heel. He thought by wearing these, he might be able to run as fast at the other kids at school, and he imagined how fun it would be to run around with the other kids at recess. He picked them up and ran straight to his mom. "These?" he said with a big smile on his face.

Amy walked over to the wall to get a price and noticed they were twenty more dollars than she had expected to spend. She got them anyway. The excitement and pure joy Ben felt was worth every dollar to Amy. Once they were done paying for the shoes, Ben put them on right away and started running around in them, staying within ten feet of his mom at all times. He was excited but was still very nervous about all the people in the mall. They stopped at the pizza store attached to the mall and got a couple of slices. Ben scarfed his down quickly, and all he wanted to do was stand up and run around. Amy picked up her pizza and ate it on the walk home. Clearly Ben had too much energy to just sit there. By the time they got home, it was dinnertime, and they were both exhausted from the day. Amy made something quick for dinner, and Ben picked out a few movies like usual. Amy had to work first thing in the morning. April was going to be there at 7:00 a.m. sharp, so they couldn't stay up too late.

The next morning when April got there, Ben ran up to her, gave her a big hug, and showed her his new shoes. Amy loved seeing that. She gave Ben a hug and headed off to work. April and Ben went inside, and he picked out the game Monopoly. They spent the rest of the day playing games and watching TV. *Pretty easy gig*, April thought.

There was only a week left till school, and Ben was starting to get his preschool jitters. He knew that once he was back at school, things were going to change. He knew he would get made fun of, and he knew he wouldn't get to see April as much. She was still going to come over and hang out on the days his mother worked late, but he wouldn't get full days with her like he did now. They didn't go to the same school, but there was a bus that went from the high school to the middle school. On the days Amy was working, April would take that bus instead of her normal bus, and she'd walk back to Ben's with him.

He felt like a new boy this year. His confidence was up, and he had a friend who liked hanging out with him. He felt on top of the world, and nothing could bring him down. He wasn't going to take shit from anyone this year. He learned that the more he rolled over and take it, the worse it was going to get. Not anymore. He knew he couldn't fight, but from all the movies he watched, he'd learned that if he stood up for himself and threw a punch, even if he got his ass kicked, they would still respect the fact that he'd stuck up for himself. Hopefully people would stop messing with him. This year wasn't going to be like the previous years. It was going to be different, and he wasn't going to let anyone mess with him.

The last week of summer flew by, and before he knew it, it was the first day back to school. It went really well. No one bothered him, and he had his first good day at school. He felt good about it, and even better, his mom worked late that day. That meant he got to hang out with April.

It wasn't till about the second week of school that it started happening again. Ben was sitting by himself and eating lunch. He was working on a list of things to do with April. The list was actually called, "A list of stuff to do with April." While he was sitting there reading it, Jason came up out of nowhere and snatched it out of his hand. Jason started reading it aloud, which infuriated Ben. All the kids were laughing and pointing. Ben demanded, "Give that back. I'm not asking you again."

Jason started laughing even harder and walked toward Ben as if he was going to punch him. Without even thinking, Ben waited for the right moment. As Jason got closer, Ben gave a right hook that sent Jason sailing to the ground. Without hesitation, Ben jumped on Jason faster than a cat pouncing on a field mouse, dropping punches on Jason's face. Jason started screaming for help and crying loudly, but none of his friends came to his aide. They stood back, stunned at what they were watching. None of them had expected this, especially Jason. By the time the lunch duty teacher heard it and saw what was going on, Ben had already landed fifteen devastating blows to Jason's face, which left him with multiple cuts that were pouring blood. The teacher ran over, and by the time she pulled Ben off, Jason was already unconscious and bleeding badly from the mouth, the nose, and open cuts on his face and forehead. Jason was rushed to the hospital.

Ben was hauled into the office, where he sat and waited for the principal and his mom to talk to him. As he sat there, he realized he had no feelings about what had just happened. No bad feelings, no sad feelings. He simply didn't feel anything. He knew he'd really hurt Jason, but he did not care at all; it meant nothing. He couldn't help but think how easy that was—and that if he hadn't been pulled off, he would have kept doing that till there was nothing left of Jason's face. What he knew was he didn't want to be bullied anymore. He was sick of it and decided that he wouldn't take it from anyone. He was going to help anyone who was in that same situation. He realized what this could mean and what he was capable of doing to someone—and he liked it. He never once thought about injuring or hurting someone who didn't do anything wrong. He looked back at all the times he'd had hateful feelings drawn out by someone who was doing something shitty to someone else. The only thing he didn't like about this was having to deal with the punishment. He felt what he did was well deserved, and just because someone else didn't like it, that didn't mean he shouldn't have done it. He was going to stand up for himself and anyone else who couldn't. Next time he wasn't going to get caught for it!

4
CHAPTER

Amy ran into the principal's office, still in her work clothes. Once she saw Ben sitting on a chair outside of the office, she wrapped her arms around him. "What happened?"

Right then, Principal Anderson walked out. He was a tall, attractive, middle-aged black man and was very well dressed. He was clean-shaven and always wore high-end suits and ties. He was bald and wore glasses, but he wore it well. Anderson was an ex-marine and ex-cop, but he'd turned to teaching four years ago and had quickly moved up the ladder. He was very educated and well spoken.

When Mr. Anderson walked toward Amy, she quickly stood up from comforting her son. "Ms. Willis, how are you? Step into my office, please." He turned around and walked into his office, not giving Amy a chance to answer.

Ben sat in the chair outside the office as his mother and Mr. Anderson went in.

"Take a seat, ma'am," Mr. Anderson said while gesturing toward the chair.

Amy was very concerned about Jason because she saw Ben didn't have a mark on him. "What happened today?"

Mr. Anderson stood up from his chair and sat on the corner of the desk, next to Amy. He pulled out his cell phone from his pocket and opened it up to photos. He explained what had happened from the perspective of the teacher who'd broken up the fight, but he didn't know what had happened beforehand to lead to it. He then handed the phone to Amy, and she started scrolling through the pictures. Her jaw dropped, and she covered her open mouth with her hand and let out a little gasp every time she flipped to a different picture. She'd had no idea Ben was capable of delivering this kind of beating. What she was looking at looked like pictures from a horror movie. Her hand trembled when she handed the phone back over. "Is he going to be all right?" she asked, worried about what the answer might be.

"Last update was about twenty minutes ago. He received a total of twenty-five stitches, mostly to close up the gash on the back of his head. They ran tests and said he is all right to go home," Mr. Anderson replied. "As far as I know, neither the cops nor the parents are pressing charges, but I am going to suspend Ben for a week."

Amy let out a light gasp and fought even harder to not break down and cry.

"In that week, I want Ben to come to school still, but with your permission he is going to spend that week with me at school every day. He will do his homework in my office, he will sit and eat his lunch, and he will have his recess in my office. This boy has some serious demons, and I want to help him, if that's okay with you."

Amy didn't know how to respond to that. She didn't like the idea of the principal prying into Ben. She didn't think Ben would say anything, but there was something in the back of her head, like a giant elephant in the room taking up all the available space, that made her paranoid. What choice did she have? If she said no, it would feed into Mr. Anderson's curiosity, or he could get mad and kick Ben out of school. If she said yes, she would have to trust that Ben wouldn't say anything about what had happened to his father. She had a little trust in Ben knowing that he did love her a lot, and she had purposely scared the shit out of him with horror stories of going to prison or foster care if they ever got caught.

Mr. Anderson was still patiently sitting and waiting for an answer while Amy took a few moments to contemplate the idea. Saying yes seemed like her best option, so she looked up at him from her chair and nodded.

"Great decision, Ms. Willis," Mr. Anderson said as he got up from sitting on the corner of the deck and went back to his chair. "I will have him do daily journals, and he will bring them home to you every night. You can read them, sign them, and send them back. It's all about routine with kids. You get any kid in a routine where he always has something to do, and he won't have time to think about anything else. He will simply do what he's been doing."

Such a smart, wise man, Amy thought. "I totally agree, Mr. Anderson. I think that is a great idea. So will he just be in here, doing his regular stuff?"

"He will be doing his school work in here, yes. But we will be spending half of the day inside and the other half outside."

"Outside? What are you going to be doing outside?"

"We are going to do exercises and nature walks. It's all related to school and his usual classes. However, now he will have his own personal teacher," Mr. Anderson explained.

"Why do you care so much? I mean no disrespect, but most schools would simply expel someone for what he did. Why are you being nice and sweet?"

"I have a soft spot for troubled kids. I used to be just like that." He sat up from his desk, eager to say what was on his mind. "I have seen worse, and I have done worse. I put my best friend in the hospital for a week when I was fifteen years old. He bought the same shoes as me, so I hit him in the head with a rock. To me at the time, it was a respect thing, and he dissed me in front of all my friends by doing that. I spent six months in juvie for that. It's where I met the man who changed my life. He is responsible for who I am today, and I will forever be grateful for that. He passed away a few years back, but when

I asked him what he wanted in return for helping me and taking me under his wing, all he wanted in return was for me to pass it on. That's all he said: pass it on. It's exactly what I intend to do."

Amy looked a bit relieved and felt a bit better about the whole thing. As she got up to say goodbye, Mr. Anderson followed her to the door to say bye to Ben. Amy gathered Ben's stuff, and they both said goodbye to Mr. Anderson and headed out the door. Amy wasn't sure how Ben was going to take the news of having to spend every day with his principal, but he didn't have a choice because she hadn't been given much of a choice! She thought, *It'll be really good for him, having a positive male role model to look up to.*

She broke the news to Ben on the way home from the school, and surprisingly enough, he liked the idea. He thought it would be cool to get outside and maybe get a start on getting in better shape. He was gaining a bit more confidence and thought maybe it was time to shed some of his baby fat.

Amy took the rest of the day off work. When they got home from the school, she thought it would be a good idea to cook a big meal and have a mother-son talk over a hot dinner. She wanted to ask right away why he'd beaten up that other boy so badly, but she also didn't want to push it too quickly and have him get upset. They got home, and Ben instantly went over to the couch and started flicking through the channels on the TV. That was odd because he had memorized all his favorite shows and the times they were on. She watched him for a minute till he stopped on the health channel. He watched the health channel for the rest of the afternoon, right up until dinner.

By the time dinner was ready, he was even hungrier than usual from watching the food channel that whole time. He walked into the kitchen and sat at the table across from his mom. He could tell she wanted to say something because she was sitting there, not eating, and staring at him.

"We need to talk about today," Amy said. "I can't believe you put that boy in the hospital. Why did you do it?"

Ben put down his fork and stared at his mother for a minute. "He deserved it," he said without an ounce of remorse. He put his head down and started eating.

"Why, though?" Amy said with a little frustration in her voice.

"Because he was a bully, and bullies deserve to be hurt."

Ben's reply gave Amy chills, but she could not fault him. She didn't want to, but deep down inside, she agreed. His father was a bully, and she thought about how much of a better life they had had since he had been gone.

After that, it was a pretty quiet dinner. How could she get mad? She would have done the same thing to a bully. She'd murdered his father for basically the same thing.

As much as she wanted to be the parent, do the right thing, and punish him for his actions, she couldn't. Deep down inside, she knew the little brat had deserved it, and if that meant her son wouldn't get bullied anymore at school, then how could she punish him?

She explained to him that it was a good thing he'd stuck up for himself, and she was glad he wasn't letting anyone push him around anymore. However, she had to explain how this looked when he did stuff like this. "If you do stuff like this and get caught for it, it looks bad on me, and eventually they will take you away from me."

Ben did not like the sound of that at all. Without his mother, he would be so lost. She was his rock, and he needed her around.

Amy stood up from the table when she was done talking and left the room while Ben finished his dinner. When she left, he whispered under his breath, "I just won't get caught next time." But he wasn't saying it to her. He was saying it to himself. He wasn't going to let anyone push him around anymore.

It was the weekend and Amy was working split shifts Saturday and Sunday. On Saturday morning when Ben woke up, Amy was already gone for work, and April was sitting on the couch and watching TV. There was a massive list of chores she'd left with April for Ben to do that would take him the entire weekend. He was upset about this because he wanted to spend all his time hanging with April. With a couple of shortcuts and half-ass jobs, he was able to get all his chores done by the end of the weekend with little time to spare. He used that time to try to impress April with telling her his fight story. She pretended to care but didn't actually care and was just amusing him.

The next day, Ben got up for school as a regular day. All he could think about was April. He couldn't wait to get home at the end of the day to hang out with her again. He wanted to tell her more about the fight he'd had. Ben thought about her all the way to school. Once he got there, he went straight to Mr. Anderson's office as instructed. He saw Mr. Anderson talking to some teachers, so he walked into the office and sat on the chair in front of Mr. Anderson's desk. A few moments later, Mr. Anderson walked in, said good morning, and sat down at his desk. He started rifling through paperwork as if he was looking for something specific, which piqued Ben's curiosity. Mr. Anderson picked them all up and bounced them off the desk top to straight them all out. He turned around in his chair and set the paperwork down on the filing cabinet behind him. Then he swung back around and folded his hands on his desk, studying Ben for a moment. He sat back in his chair while Ben sat there, waiting for instruction.

"Ben," Mr. Anderson said with a furrowed brow while sitting upright in his chair. "Do you have a safe place?"

Ben was a little confused by the question.

"You know, like a place where you feel comfortable, safe. A place that is yours and nobody else's."

Ben nodded his head and quietly answered. "My bedroom."

"Okay, great," Mr. Anderson replied. "Your bedroom! And do people ever just walk into your bedroom whenever they want? Like your mom, or if family was over?"

"No," Ben replied. He was still confused about where the principal was going with this.

"And you would probably be upset if they did, wouldn't you?" Mr. Anderson asked.

"Sure." Ben shrugged, still not sure where this was going.

"Okay, well think of my office as my comfort place. I do not like people in my office while I am not in here. Much like you wouldn't like people in your room when you are not there. Especially if they just invited themselves in. So from now on, Ben—and this applies to life as well—don't just walk into people's places or invade their personal space. Always wait to be invited. If I'm not here in the morning, you are more than welcome to pull up a chair in front of my office door and start working on your school work till I arrive. No more just sitting there and waiting for me to give you instruction. Do you understand what I mean? I'm not angry because you didn't know, but this is a respect thing, and it's what's to be expected from a mature human being."

Ben felt a little embarrassed, but in all honesty he had no idea what he'd done was wrong. Now that it was explained to him, it did seem pretty reasonable. "That makes sense," Ben said.

"Good. Now, let's get started." Ben opened up his bag to grab all his school work, but Mr. Anderson stopped him. "Don't worry about your books right now," he said as he stood up from his deck and looked outside and up at the clouds. "We are going to get to know one another today. Outside. Looks like the rain might hold off for a bit, and there is a gully down there we are going to hike."

"Hike?" Ben replied with the kind of look on his face one would get from a child when offering him an apple over a bunch of candy.

Mr. Anderson knew Ben didn't like that idea, but he didn't care. "Get up. Let's go. I know you don't want to do this, but you have to," Mr. Anderson said in a joking but serious kind of way with a half smile.

Ben stood up and put on his coat. Mr. Anderson explained to him that the morning was the best time to go for a hike. All the smells came to life in the morning. All the animals were waking up and running around. When the fog lifted and the sun was trying its hardest to break through, it was such a beautiful and peaceful experience. By the time they made it to the doors to go outside, Ben was pretty pumped to do this. It sounded like a cool experience.

Mr. Anderson told Ben about how when he was a marine, he would have to do camping trips like this in the middle of the jungle or in the middle of the mountains. Ben seemed very interested in these outdoor stories, so as they were walking through the football field to get to the woods, Mr. Anderson told Ben about the one time when his platoon had been stranded in the Congo jungle for three weeks and had to survive off the vegetation, trapping animals when they could.

They made it to a big opening in the woods, and it was beautiful. Ben didn't get out much outside of school and wasn't used to seeing this kind of scenery—other than when he and his mother had dumped his dad's body. This reminded him of it, but it wasn't a negative feeling. It was calming, and he took peace knowing his dad was laid to rest surrounded by such beauty.

Ben was looking around when he noticed a structure built against the tree. He instantly walked over to it and started checking it out. That was exactly what Mr. Anderson had hoped he would do. Ben noticed that it had an opening on the one side.

"It's called a lean-to," Mr. Anderson said as he walked up beside Ben. "These have been built for centuries. It's an easy structure to build, and they are durable. They can keep you warm at night and keep the rain off your back. I am going to teach you things that you can use your entire life while we are out here."

"Did you build this one?" asked Ben.

"Yup, in just an afternoon. You are going to build one just like it."

Ben was excited about the idea of building one, and he checked out the structure in front of him to get a good idea of how it was built.

"Notice the V-shaped sticks I used at both ends to support the main branch in the middle?" Mr. Anderson said as he watched Ben analyze the structure. A few moments went by, and Ben started gathering branches and snapping them down the size. Mr. Anderson wanted to help but also wanted to see how well Ben would do on his own. If he noticed Ben having trouble, he would explain to him what he was doing wrong and how to do it right. But Ben caught on pretty quick, and by lunchtime he had a perfectly livable lean-to.

When Ben was finished building, Mr. Anderson explained how there were many different ways to build a lean-to. They heard the bell ring for lunch. Ben was hungry and asked if they were heading up for lunch soon. Mr. Anderson got a big smile on his face and said no. Ben was starving, and Mr. Anderson saying no pissed off Ben a bit. Mr. Anderson walked over to his lean-to and pulled out a basket. He brought it over to Ben, set it on the ground, and took a seat beside it. Ben stood there observing while Mr. Anderson cleared a spot about a foot and a half from the opening of Ben's lean-to. He got it to where it was a round circle of dirt and started filling it all in with smaller stones he had collected. He put the bigger rocks to the outside of the circle to encase the fire-pit, except for the side that was facing the opening of the tepee. He put the gravel in the middle, covering the dirt, and had them coming out of the firepit toward the opening.

"I am going to show you how to heat your lean-to and cook with that same heat. Gather as many twigs and strips of bark as you can find."

Ben did just that. He came back and set all his stuff down beside the big pile of wood Mr. Anderson had collected.

"All right, Ben. I'm going to show you how to make a fire. First, I want to explain something to you. I am teaching you these things because I think you are a good kid, and I believe that everyone should attain these basic survival skills. But these skills are not to be used for anything else than survival. Do you understand that?" Mr. Anderson said as he set up the firewood in the pit in the shape of a tepee.

Ben didn't answer. He simply nodded yes and continued to watch intently.

"Okay, good. Let's get this fire started," Mr. Anderson said as he lit all the bark and twigs he'd stuffed inside the tepee. "You'll notice the strips of bark I put in there go up like paper. The best way to start a fire is dried bark and twigs or dry grass. Then you build this tepee structure and stuff all that in the middle of the tepee, and you will have a fire going in no time." Mr. Anderson pulled out a white tablecloth, laid it flat, and then pulled out all sorts of things. Little chunks of beef, chicken, cheese, crackers, and some soft drinks. "I thought we could have lunch down here and get to know each other a bit better. What do you say?" Mr. Anderson grabbed the frying pan and greased it up.

"Yeah, that's cool," Ben replied.

It took a bit longer then Ben expected, but after a bit, Mr. Anderson grabbed a stick and cleared a bunch of coals off a small part of the rock bed he'd made. When he did that, he forced the smaller coals to slip between the rock bed, creating more heat. He set the frying pan down on it, and within a minute the butter was melted and spattering. Ben then realized why the principal had left the bigger rocks out and made a stone bed coming out of the firepit. It was so he could pull his frying pan out of the coals but still kept it on the warm stones.

They fried up all the meat, and during that time, Ben told Mr. Anderson a little bit about himself. Mr. Anderson told Ben how he was an ex-marine, what kind of stuff he'd done, and where he'd traveled.

Mr. Anderson wanted this to be a trust-building day, and he didn't really care if Ben didn't say much this time. He was fine with telling stories from his past and making Ben laugh and feel comfortable around him.

Ben told him a little about April but didn't give too much detail. After lunch, they spent a few more hours building and gathering before heading back up to the school. For the rest of the week, they spent half the day inside doing school work and the other half outside playing sports or learning more survival skills. The week seemed to fly by, and neither one of them was ready for it to be over.

Mr. Anderson didn't have much of a life outside of work. He lived an isolated life and did a lot of reading. He'd been in the marines from the age of eighteen to thirty-four, when he was honorably discharged. He then became a cop for ten years and had retired with a full pension from the military and police force. He wasn't quite ready to retire yet and decided to get into teaching. He was seemingly a model citizen and perfect role model, but everyone had a past, and everyone had demons. His were far worse than any normal person, and for a long time he'd tried fixing his problems by drowning his emotions in alcohol. That was ultimately the demise of his marriage. When he'd been in the military, he'd been forced to completely annihilate a small village that was interrupting a pipeline project. From that moment on, they were the platoon people would call to exterminate anyone who stood in the way of what they called progression. Anderson was paid to slaughter the innocent so the higher powers could make more money. They would go into a village, and before long most of the men started raping the women and keeping them around as their personal slaves. These men had gone into this with good intentions, but it was the rules of war that broke them and made them products of their environment.

When Anderson came back, he became a heavy drinker and was forced into early retirement from the police force. Shortly after that, his wife had left him, and ever since then he'd been keeping clean and doing his job in the hopes to find forgiveness—and to forgive himself. He never took part in the raping of the women, but he felt just as guilty for murdering them. The village men would put up a small fight, but they didn't stand a chance, and with almost no resistance Anderson's unit swiftly moved in and cleared the area.

Mr. Anderson never talked about any of that outside his therapist's office. He told some stories to Ben, but they were the funny ones or the ones where they'd taken on gunfire but had not engaged into any type of combat besides shooting into the trees. Ben was interested in every word Mr. Anderson said.

The following Friday, Ben was sitting in Mr. Anderson's office when he asked if he could come back the next week, so they could keep doing the same thing. All of Ben's assignments improved and he was learning lots from being outside every day. Mr. Anderson noticed a difference in his own work and state of mind, and he thought it could be a good idea. There was still so much they both wanted to learn from each other, and Ben's work was improving quite a bit. They decided to do it again for another couple of weeks but could only do it for half days and weekends due to Mr. Andersons day to day responsibilities, and if Ben's marks improved a lot and he became a better student, then they would think about long-term arrangements.

A couple of weeks into it, Amy asked Mr. Anderson to spend dinner with them. Amy was busy with work and hadn't had much time to get the details from Ben. Plus, every time she asked Ben how school was going, he would give her one-word answers. She saw a big improvement at home and in Ben's school work, and she wanted to also show her appreciation by cooking a nice, home-cooked meal. She knew Mr. Anderson lived alone, and she thought he would like this a lot.

The dinner was set up for the following Friday. Amy didn't have to work that day, and she wanted to cook her son a nice dinner for doing so well. Amy dropped off Ben at school and came in to confirm with Mr. Anderson.

When she left, Ben noticed that Mr. Anderson was in a better mood then most days, and all day they just sat in the cafeteria watching movies and playing card games, which were activities they'd never done before. He saw those as being a waste of time.

Ben saw Mr. Anderson as superhuman. He saw him as flawless, able to do anything. He had zero vulnerability, like a superhero. Ben started looking up to Mr. Anderson and thought, *That's the man I want to grow up to be like.*

For the rest of the week, all they did was play games and kill time. It wasn't the same as the last couple of weeks at all. Anderson was more lenient, demanding less school work. It seemed that the invite he'd received from Amy was going to his head. Every time Ben would bring up his mom, Mr. Anderson would get a big smile on his face. He said she was a beautiful woman and was smart, and Ben should listen to everything she said. All Ben could think was, *if you only knew.*

He didn't like the way Mr. Anderson had been acting since Amy had invited him to dinner. He wasn't that strong, stern man Ben had somewhat feared and greatly respected.

He was weak and bubbly. Ben hated it. Even the secretary said something about Mr. Anderson's happy demeanor. Ben had a bad feeling about this and feared losing this relationship.

On Friday when Ben showed up for school, he sat out front of Mr. Anderson's office, pulled out some school work, and started working on it while he waited. He looked up at the clock and saw Mr. Anderson was running late. He started hoping that he wasn't going to show up because he was sick or something. Maybe he would have to cancel dinner tonight. Ben didn't know why, but he had a bad feeling about Mr. Anderson coming over for dinner tonight.

Half an hour later, Mr. Anderson walked in the office and walked straight over to Ben. "You could have gone into my office, son," Mr. Anderson said with a big smile as he opened up the door. "I trust you."

Ben stood up from the chair, walked into the office, set up his book, and started working. Mr. Anderson sat across from him and looked at Ben like he wanted to say something but wasn't sure whether or not he should. This annoyed Ben to the point where he stopped working, looked up at Mr. Anderson, and waited for him to say what was on his mind.

Mr. Anderson started asking Ben about dinner, and about Amy. He wanted to know if she had a boyfriend and what kind of flowers she liked. By the end of the day, Ben felt like he had done nothing but answer questions about his mom. That was a new thing for him to experience. He really loved his mother, and he was angry at the thought of Mr. Anderson lusting after her.

On the walk home, Ben thought more and more about Mr. Anderson's questions. The more he thought about them, the more it pissed him off. He felt very conflicted. On one hand, he had this awesome mentor who would be a great father figure. On the other hand, he didn't want anyone coming in between him and his mom. When his dad had been around, Ben had received no attention from his mom. He would do anything to make it so that didn't happen again.

When he got home, his mother was in the kitchen, getting the prep work done for dinner. "Hey, sweetie. Come give Mommy a hand."

Ben set down his gym bag, took off his shoes, and walked into the kitchen. Amy was all dressed up and had on more makeup than she needed.

"Mom, please don't date Mr. Anderson."

Amy laughed. "Honey, I am not going to date your teacher. He's just coming over for dinner tonight so we can talk more about you. And I want to show our appreciation for everything he is doing for you. Besides, he's not my type." She playfully winked and giggled before going back to emptying the pasta noodles for the macaroni salad into the strainer Ben held.

He felt relieved at hearing this from his mom. He thought it was over, and he didn't have to worry anymore about anyone leaving him. Mr. Anderson was going to stay where he was, and his mom was going to stay where she was. Everything was good.

About an hour later, Amy was finishing the last bit of what was left to set out for dinner. Ben was sitting on the couch and watching TV when he heard a few knocks on the door. He got up, and because of what his mom had said, he was now excited to see Mr. Anderson. He ran up to the door, grabbed the knob, and swung it open. Mr. Anderson stood there with a bottle of wine in one hand and chocolates and flowers in the other. He smelled really good and was wearing a suit he'd never worn to school before. This one was more shiny and bright with pinstripes. The suits he normally wore were boring and usually just one color.

"Hey, buddy. How are ya?" Mr. Anderson said with lots of energy.

"I'm all right. How are you, Mr. Anderson?" Ben said with a big smile.

"Na, call me John, my boy. At school I'm Mr. Anderson!"

Just then, Amy walked into the foyer. She had a spatula in one hand and an oven mitt on the other. "Hey, John. Come on in. Dinner is almost ready." Then she turned around and went back into the kitchen.

Completely ignoring Ben, John followed Amy into the kitchen. After setting the bottle of wine down, he walked over to Amy and handed her the flowers and chocolates. Amy was surprised at this and accepted the gesture to be nice, but she didn't like the idea of him giving her flowers and chocolates. She instantly started talking about Ben to try to reinforce the reason for John being there. However, John kept changing the subject to more personal stuff about her. He kept asking her what she did in her free time and whether she had considered a relationship since her husband's passing.

These questions made her feel very uncomfortable. Amy had started seeing someone who always came into her work. It wasn't serious, and she didn't want to tell Ben about it, but she had been on a couple of dates and kind of liked the guy. She knew what John was doing, but she was worried that if she was straight up with him and told him she was not interested, he might treat Ben differently at school. She thought it was best to get through the night and then avoid talking to him in person, sticking to phone calls when they needed to contact each other about Ben. She needed to get through the night.

During the meal, Amy kept bringing up Ben's schooling, but John would quickly answer the question and then change the subject. It was a complete waste of time for Amy, and she realized her good deed was backfiring.

By the end of the dinner, Amy was more than ready to hurry John out the door. She did the cleanup and then made some excuse that they had to get to bed early because they had stuff to do in the morning. John took the hint, gathered his stuff, and headed for the door. Ben was already watching TV on the couch and wasn't getting up for anyone. All he did was wave goodbye to John, and he didn't take his eyes off the TV.

Amy walked John to the door and was saying good night when John made a move and tried kissing her. Amy quickly pulled away with an angry look on her face. "This dinner wasn't an invitation into my pants, John. This was so I could learn how my son was doing in school."

John smiled, and right before he went in for another kiss, he said, "Playing hard to get, I see."

This time instead of pulling away, she stood her ground and pushed him back. That was hard for her to do because he was twice the size of her. "I started seeing someone at work. I'm sorry. I would have told you when you gave me the flowers, but it's not something I'm ready for Ben to find out yet."

This upset John. He'd thought this was a date, and during the past week, he had a mental image of them and what it would be like to be with her. He'd held on to that so tightly that he'd started to believe it was not only possible but a given. It had already happened just by her inviting him over for dinner. To hear she was seeing someone was a complete shock and heartbreak.

"What?" he replied, as if he thought he'd heard wrong.

"I'm sorry. I had no idea you felt like this. I wouldn't have in—"

John cut her off by slamming his fist off the door trim. "You wouldn't have what? Dolled yourself up every time you came to the school to see me? Wouldn't have complimented me so many times? Or invited me over for dinner? No, I see how it is. Get what you want from me, and that's it."

"No, that's not it at all," Amy said as she stepped out the door and closed it behind her so Ben couldn't hear. "The only fucking reason I invited you over for dinner is to show my appreciation for what you are doing for my child. He has benefited so much over the last couple of weeks, and I've noticed amazing improvements at home too."

John rolled his eyes and looked away with a half-ass smile on his face.

Amy continued. "I hope this doesn't affect your and Ben's relationship. And I truly am sorry if I gave you the impression I wanted something more than just being friends."

"Friends?" John laughed. He turned and walked back to his car. "Yeah, don't worry about Ben. I'll keep up on my end of the deal."

Amy had no idea what he meant by that, but she wasn't going to press it, because he was leaving. That was what she wanted him to do most. When she turned around, Ben was standing in the doorway when she came back in.

"What was that about?" Ben asked.

Amy lied and said he was upset about something at work.

Ben knew something was up but chose not to shed any light on it, and he headed back to the couch to watch more TV.

Amy started feeling really guilty the more she thought about it. This was the first time things were going well for Ben, and she might have ruined it by having the man who was helping him over for dinner. When he'd left, John had been very mad. She thought that if worse came to worst, she would simply put Ben in another school.

Amy went on with her night and tried not to think about it anymore. She and Ben had plans to walk down to the video store, rent some movies, and get some snacks. She didn't want to ruin that with a bad mood.

She finished cleaning, and they headed down to the video store. Ben was on a mission to rent a very scary movie and then a very funny movie to watch afterward. Amy didn't really care what movies they rented; she simply enjoyed hanging out with him. He was going to be fourteen in a few months, and she thought he wouldn't want anything to do with her when he got to that age. They both fell asleep on the couch together watching the movie.

It was about two in the morning when they were both woken up by the sound of someone knocking on the door. They were light knocks, but they started getting heavier and louder. Amy peeked out the front window and saw John sanding there, one hand on the door frame holding himself up. The hand he was using to knock on the door had a bottle of whiskey in it; it was half gone. She hurried Ben off to bed, went to the door, took a deep breath, and opened it. The second she opened it far enough, he stuck his foot in so she couldn't close it. She noticed him do that and had a bad feeling this wasn't going to end well.

"Why am I not good enough for you?" John mumbled.

"I never said that, John. And what are you doing, coming to my house this late at night? I thought you were a recovering alcoholic, by the way," Amy said as she pointed to the bottle.

"You know what? We are who we are. I have come to realize that over the last few months. I can't hide it anymore. I am a monster."

"What? What are you even talking about?" Amy snapped.

John stood there for a second with a dead look in his face. His eyes were glossy from the booze, and the lack of emotion and expression on his face was so haunting that Amy tried shutting the door. It almost closed, but his foot stopped it. Amy started slamming her body against the door, trying to hurt his foot so he would pull it out, but it didn't work. He timed it perfectly so when she went to slam into the door again, he reached through the opening of the door and grabbed her by the throat. Completely helpless at this point, she had no choice but to stop resisting and let him in; otherwise, she was going to pass out from lack of oxygen.

When she moved out of the way, he quickly entered and closed the door behind him, still squeezing Amy's throat. It was a matter of seconds, and Amy felt herself completely slip away. She came to about ten minutes later, sitting at the kitchen table with her hands tied to the chair on which she was sitting.

5
CHAPTER

Amy was so confused at first and didn't know where she was or what was going on. Then she looked up and saw that dead stare. John was sitting in front of her on a chair. He had the chair turned around, and he rested his head on the back of it. His chin was buried into the bend of his arm, and his other arm dangled down by his side with the bottle of booze hanging from his fingertips. He brought the bottle up to his lips, took a mouthful, and swallowed it down with almost no expression.

"It didn't have to come to this, Amy. You have always wanted me, I just need to make you see it." John stood up, unbuttoned his blue shirt, and threw it to the floor. "You will love me after tonight."

His face went from calm to angry, and he lunged at Amy, grabbing her by the arms.

"I'm going to make you love me!" he yelled in Amy's face.

All Amy could think about was how Ben was in the next room. She couldn't imagine what John would do to him if he saw what John was doing to her. She prayed he stayed sleeping.

When John grabbed her by the arms, he leaned in for an aggressive, wet, and disgustingly sloppy kiss. When he pulled away from her, his hands went down to the tape on her wrists, and he started undoing it. He took a deep breath and whispered in her ear, "If you shout, I will hurt you. If Ben comes out here, I will hurt you both!"

John leaned in a bit farther and started kissing Amy's neck. It took all she had to not kick and scream at the top of her lungs. She knew someone would hear her. Her neighbor's house was so close to hers that they could hear them watching TV sometimes. But she knew if she did, Ben would come out, and even though she was afraid for her life, she feared more what John would do. What would it do to Ben if he saw his mother getting raped? She bit down on her tongue and held back any fight she had left in her.

John started working his way down to Amy's chest, breathing heavy and groping her. She felt so violated and couldn't believe this was happening. All she could smell was his breath and his sweat. She decided she would take it and hope that he'd leave when he was done. Suddenly, he flipped the chair over. Amy's head went crashing to the floor, temporarily knocking her out.

When she came to a few minutes later, he had already torn off the restraints he'd made and had flipped her on her stomach. There was a small pool of blood on the floor from her head injury, and she was face down in it. She felt every single touch, every kiss. She felt his hot breath on her back. It was by far the worst thing she had ever been through, but like an unstoppable freight train, all the bad stuff she had ever done came rushing into her brain. It was so vivid to her. The memories were right there, and she could reach out and change them as they played in her head over and over again. The whole situation was torturous for her, and there wasn't a damn thing she could do to stop it. She started thinking she might deserve this from all the shitty things she had done. It was as if karma was finally catching up to her, and she had to take it.

Right then, she heard the sound of a door opening. She closed her eyes tightly and hoped that the sound was just in her head. She opened them back up and looked in the direction of Ben's room. She saw his door was open a crack, and when her eyes focused, she saw Ben through the crack of the door, sitting on the floor with deep fear in his eyes. She made eye contact with him for a minute before she passed out from the pain, and all she could do was shake her head no.

Ben had to sit there and watch his mother get raped, and there wasn't anything he could do about it. John was such a big man that Ben wouldn't be able to do a thing to him. He was in complete shock. This man was so important to him. He was more than just a principal. He was a friend—and Ben's only friend at that.

Ben shut the door and sat up against it. He felt like such a coward and couldn't believe he didn't have the courage to help his mom. This made him feel bad. He figured pretty quickly that his only recourse had to be sneaky. As he sat there listening to the sound of his mother getting raped right outside of his door, he started thinking of other ways to get back at John. He couldn't let him get away with this.

Then it went silent. Ben couldn't hear anything, but the silence was broken by the sound of footsteps walking around. He heard the front door open and then close. Ben sat there and waited for a minute to see if he could hear anything else. It was dead silent. He stood up, grabbed the door knob, and turned it. Before he pulled the door open, the thought of seeing his mom dead on the floor came into his head and hit him hard. He started crying. This was a possibility, and he couldn't imagine what he would do if she was no longer around. He started getting a feeling he'd never had before. It was overwhelming, and he felt it throughout his entire body. He could feel the fear slowly fade, replaced with a feeling of rage and anger. A feeling of revenge.

He flung open the door and ran over to his mom, who was lying in a pool of her blood. He flipped her over on her back and started lightly slapping her in the face and shaking her till she came to. Amy jumped up in a panic because she thought John was still there. It took her a few seconds to catch her balance; she acted like she had the feet of a newborn calf. Once she fully came to, she looked around and saw that he was gone. She ran to the door and locked it. It was only when she felt safe and knew he was gone that she allowed herself to fall to the ground and start crying. This enraged Ben even more. All he could do was stand on the other side of the room, staring at his mom, helpless and with pain and sadness filling his eyes.

After a bit, she stood up, wiped the tears from her face, and sat at the kitchen table. She sat there with a blank look on her face, staring into the abyss. Ben had no idea what to do or how she would react if he said anything, but he couldn't take it anymore. He walked over to Amy and wrapped his arms around her. She snapped out of it, hugged him back, and apologized for what had happened. Ben didn't understand why she was saying sorry to him. It was Mr. Anderson who should be feeling sorry, and Ben couldn't wait to make sure he did.

He helped his mother up and took her over to the couch so she could lie down. He put on a funny movie, hoping it would help a bit. It took about five minutes, and Amy fell asleep on the couch. Ben sat by her side all night and didn't get any sleep. All he could think about was what he was going to do to Mr. Anderson. It needed to happen that evening, but he had to do it in a way where he would not get caught. It was clear now that he could never leave his mother's side, and he had to always be there to protect her.

Amy woke up at about nine o'clock to the smell of Ben cooking breakfast. He'd never cooked before, but since they'd gotten the internet, he had been looking up all sorts of things on Google. This morning he'd googled how to make bacon and eggs.

Amy wasn't hungry at all when she woke, but she managed to choke it down. Her stubbornness to not let John ruin anything helped her eat.

"Are you okay, Mom?" Ben asked.

"Yes, dear. I'll be fine. We can never mention this to anyone, okay?" Amy commanded.

Ben was happy to hear this. He didn't want to go to the police. He didn't want John to sit in jail. He wanted John to die. He wanted his life. He wanted to feel the life leave John's body, and he wanted it to happen tonight.

For the rest of the morning, Ben planned a very simple way to get back at John. It was something easy that wasn't going to get him busted. The plan was to wait till his mother fell asleep. She could not know about this. *She's been through enough.* He would sneak out, walk to Mr. Anderson's, and wait till he fell asleep. It was a small town, and most people didn't lock their doors. Ben was banking on that; otherwise, he would have to find an open window or break in through the basement somehow. Once he was inside, he would get a kitchen knife and sneak to his bedroom. Once he was in the bedroom, he would sneak over to the bed and plunge the knife directly into Mr. Anderson's heart. Then he'd turn around and leave. He watched a couple of videos on the internet on how to leave a perfectly clean crime scene, took a few pointers, and applied them to what he was doing.

That entire Saturday, he planned out what he was going to do, right down to the first step he took on the monster's property. Amy was in a daze the whole day, which infuriated Ben even more. She simply lay on the couch all day, drifting in and out of consciousness while watching TV. Ben was very conflicted. He wanted to take his mom to the hospital, but he knew that if they did go, the doctors would ask a lot of questions and would involve the police. If Amy said who did it, Ben wouldn't have a chance to kill John before the police picked him up. And he really wanted John to die. Jail wasn't good enough.

Ben was so angry about what he'd seen this man do to his mom, but what was almost as bad was the fact that this man meant a lot to him. After just a few weeks of spending every weekday with John, Ben looked up to him and saw him as a better father figure and role model than his real dad had ever been. However, Ben couldn't put his own selfish needs in front of his mother's health and wellness.

John lived a fifteen-minute bike ride away, and that was how Ben planned on getting there.

Night fell, and Ben repeatedly went over the scenario. All he could do was hope that it went exactly to plan, because it was clearer to him now that he needed to be around to protect his mother.

Amy fell asleep on the couch around eight o'clock, which was perfect because Ben wanted to be there before John went to bed to witness he was actually home before Ben committed to breaking in.

Once he knew his mother was out for the rest of the night, he went into his room, grabbed his gear, and started packing it into a gym bag. There wasn't much in it: a toque. A pair of old sneakers with duct tape covering the pattern on the bottom of the shoes. A pair of his mother's kitchen gloves.

He gathered all that up, dressed in black clothes, and quietly crept out of the house. Ben grabbed his bike, tore off the reflectors and stuck them in his bag, and pushed his bike to the end of the driveway. Just before jumping on, he looked back at his home. The thought of his mother in there hurting reassured him that he had no choice but to do this. He turned around and pedaled down the sidewalk, trying to stay in the shadows of the trees.

When he arrived in front of John's house, he couldn't believe how fast the ride had gone by. His mind must have been racing because it felt like it was a few minutes. He nervously stood outside for a good ten minutes before getting the nerve to go through with it. He started sneaking up the side of the house, got to the backyard, and crept up on the back deck to get close to the window. Ben took a look inside to see John, and sure enough, just as he'd hoped, John was sitting in the lounge chair in the living room, watching TV with a bottle of booze that was almost completely gone. Ben knew it wasn't the same bottle from last night because it was a different bottle shape. He sat out there and watched John for another half hour before he saw him move at all. All John did was grab the bottle, put it to his lips, and chug as much as he possibly could before almost throwing up.

Ben almost felt kind of bad. He saw the same loneliness and pain in him that he saw in his mom. Then he thought about the pain John had caused, and those feelings of remorse went away.

Ben couldn't see too well from the position he was in, so he had to relocate. Now that he knew John was home, he could prepare for what was about to happen. He ran to the backyard, to the back corner where there was a bunch of trees. While somewhat hidden, he changed into his killing clothes. He changed his shoes, put on the toque, and then put on the gloves. He slowly walked back up to the house, but this time he needed to see whether John was sleeping, which would mean going to the window on the side of the house where he was more exposed and could easily be seen if someone walked by. It was about ten o'clock, and Ben relied on the idea that it was too late for people to be out walking around. He put the gym bag back on his bike and crept up the side of the house to the window he wanted to look through. Ben was good at being aware of his surrounding, and he kept a close eye on the streets. He got to the window and slowly lifted his head to take a peek. John's mouth was wide open, his head was back, and he had rapid eye movements. He was out cold. Ben ran around to the back of the house and to the deck. This time instead of going to the window, he went to the back patio door. With any luck, it would be unlocked. It was. *So far, so good,* he thought. He took his first step inside the house. It was very overwhelming, but a good overwhelming. It was like he knew he was doing something wrong and still wanted to do it. But what made it twisted was he wanted to do it despite his personal feelings. He loved the idea that he was about to commit a brutal murder.

He tiptoed to the drawers, looked for the knife drawer, and came across a knife block. He carefully lifted each knife to see which one was the biggest. He came to the big chef's knife and thought that would be the best tool to use. There was one more knife in the block he never looked at but had to lift due to OCD: the carving fork. He pulled it out of the block and stared at it for a minute, almost like he was in a trance. He stuck the carving fork in his back pocket, picked up the big knife, and slowly crept toward the recliner in which John was sleeping.

When he walked up and was standing over John, he stood there, analyzing John's face. For the first time, he noticed all the imperfections on his face, every wrinkle and freckle. Before that moment, Ben had seen John as more than human, stronger than anyone, someone with zero vulnerability and who could do anything. He didn't see that in John's face tonight. What he saw was a man who did have faults and insecurities. That man was no different from Ben's own father. The longer Ben stared at John's face, the angrier he got. He wanted John to see his face. He wanted John to know he was the one killing him. He positioned himself on the left side and stood by John's knees so that when he plunged the knife in him, John would be able to see who it was, and he would know why.

Ben took a deep breath in and dropped the knife down on his chest so hard it broke the handle right off. John instantly flailed, knocking Ben to the ground. Ben hurried to his feet, grabbing the carving fork from his back pocket and thinking that he'd missed the heart and that John was coming in for an attack, but by the time he stood up, John was lying on the floor dead. Ben had never seen so much blood in his life. It was leaking out of John so quickly. Ben took a minute to gather his thoughts. All he could do was stare at the body and all the blood. It was fascinating to him. There was something he found oddly satisfying about watching the big blood spot on the carpet get even bigger.

He finally snapped out of it. It was time to go. He took a quick look around to see whether he'd left any tracks or any other evidence that might get him caught, and he didn't see anything. He went out the back door and headed to the backyard to change back into his clothes. Then he cautiously slinked down the driveway, looking around to see whether anyone was watching or might have seen. He made it to the end of the driveway and saw he was in the clear, so he pedaled his way home like he was being chased. All he could think about was getting home and being in the safety of his home, with his mother.

It only took a couple of minutes before he was back in his own driveway. He biked up to it without even slowing down, got to the front door, and slammed on the brakes. He jumped off, set his bike up, and ran inside. Amy was still sleeping on the couch, and a movie played on the TV. Ben quietly went to his room and stashed his gym bag under his bed. Then he headed back out to the living room to cuddle up on the couch with his mom.

The next day, they both woke up on the couch. Amy woke up earlier than Ben and started cooking breakfast. She seemed to be in a better mood; her normal movements suggested that her pain was going away too. Ben woke up to the smell of food cooking, and he sat at the kitchen table.

"Good morning, honey. Hungry?" Amy said with a big smile while she flipped the sizzling bacon in the pan.

"Yes, please," Ben said, staring blankly.

When the food was fully cooked, she brought a plate over to Ben and handed it to him.

They were just finishing up breakfast when they heard a bunch of sirens and saw a bunch of emergency vehicles flying down the main road. Amy was a curious person, so instantly she jumped up from the table and ran to the front door. She opened it and stood there, listening to see how far away the sirens were. A few of their neighbors were doing the same thing, and Ben could hear his mother and a couple of the ladies yelling at one another from across the street. It was a small town where everyone knew everyone, so people would usually gossip and come up with their own theories of what had happened.

They were out there talking for an hour before Amy came back into the house. When she walked in, she didn't see Ben there, so she walked over to his room. He wasn't in there either. She went to see whether he was out back when she noticed the basement door open just a little bit and the light was on. Ben hadn't been down there since the night he'd moved upstairs, and that made Amy very curious. She quietly sneaked down the steps to catch Ben doing whatever it was he was doing. It was something she would soon regret doing.

As she walked down the steps, she could see Ben kneeling on the ground, hunched over something.

"Ben," Amy said sharply. Ben's body jumped from the sudden sound of his mother's voice. "What are you doing down here?"

She nervously sauntered over to him, and as she came up beside him, she saw he had a hole dug in the dirt. He was burying a plastic bag. "What's in the bag? Amy demanded.

Ben sat there silent the entire time, looking down at the half-filled hole. He didn't know what to say or what to do, so he slowly started filling in the hole again.

Amy positioned herself in front of him and knelt on the ground. Ben would not look her in the face. He simply stared at the bag in the hole and slowly kept pushing dirt over it. Amy went to grab the bag, but Ben stopped her. He looked her straight in the eye. "Don't open that bag, Mom. Everything is fine."

When she looked into his eyes, she noticed something she had never seen before. A cold and empty look, as if she was looking into a black hole. It gave her goose bumps, and with that, she did not want to know what was in the bag. *It's best to let it be,* she thought. Deep down inside, she didn't want to know what was in the bag. She couldn't deal with that truth. Ben filled in the rest of the hole. Amy, horrified, got up and hurried up the steps. She kept telling herself that she was overthinking it—that it was probably nothing of any importance in the bag. Maybe it was a new shirt she'd gotten him that he'd ruined and he was too afraid to tell her about it.

A few moments later, Ben walked up the steps. He closed the basement door behind him and headed toward the bathroom. His eyes never left the floor as he dragged his feet across the ground, making a *thud* sound when his heel hit the hardwood. Amy watched as he passed by. A few moments later, the silence was broken by the sound of the shower turning on and the water hitting the tub.

Amy went out on the front porch to see whether any of the neighbors were out there and whether they had heard anything yet. When she walked out, she saw that not only were the ladies outside, but they stood off to the side of the road in a group across the street. They all noticed Amy standing there at the same time, and without hesitation they turned and scurried across the road like a bunch of frightened rabbits.

"Amy, did you hear?" one lady said, looking like she was going to explode if she didn't get it out. Before Amy could even answer, the lady said, "John Anderson was murdered in his sleep last night!"

Amy couldn't help but feel a little satisfied at hearing that. "How did it happen?" she asked.

They went dead silent and dropped their gazes to the ground. It was quiet for a few seconds until an older lady looked up at Amy and explained how he'd been stabbed to death with his own kitchen knife while he was sleeping in his recliner. A single stab wound directly to the heart. He'd died almost instantly.

"Oh my god. That is horrible. Do they have any witnesses or leads?"

All the women nervously looked around at one another. "No one knows," said the older lady. "Although it's a pretty small town. Someone will slip up. Just a matter of time."

"Well, in that time, let's hope this murderous freak doesn't strike again!" another lady said.

Amy walked back up to the house from the street. She knew it was Ben. She simply didn't know whether to bring it up to him or pretend like it had never happened. After all, there wasn't any proof by the sound of it, and unless she heard it from Ben's mouth, it could have been anyone for all she was concerned. On one hand, she hated John for what he had done to her and couldn't help but feel relief. But on the other hand, she knew what it was like to take a life and how it would haunt her for the rest of her life. She didn't want her son suffering the same fate. She walked back in the house. Just like any other day, Ben was sitting on the end of the couch, watching and laughing at his favorite TV shows. *Maybe he didn't do it*, she thought. *Maybe it is just a crazy coincidence.* She hated Ben's dad and wouldn't change the fact that she'd killed him if she could, but after she'd killed him, she was not the same for days. Ben was acting completely normal. She figured there was no way he would be acting normal if he had just murdered someone. She stood there, analyzed him for a bit, and concluded that there was no way it was him. He was acting much too normal. Whatever he was burying in the basement must have been nothing at all. She could stop worrying about it now.

By that evening, the news about John's brutal murder had swept through the whole town. John was known only as the man he'd pretended to be. The hero vet, the legendary teacher who could teach anyone, and the great principal who cared for every student and loved his job. Everyone came out that night to put flowers on his front yard and pay their respects. There was a large gathering in front of his house. Amy joined her neighbors so as to not look suspicious or gain any attention. She didn't want to, but she did. She couldn't believe how many people had bought into his lying bullshit—just like she had. It made her mad that so many people stood there and told funny stories about him. So many people were fooled and came to pay their respects to him. It took everything she had not to lash out and tell everyone what a big piece of shit he really was and that he deserved every piece of what he got.

Amy didn't allow Ben to come to the gathering even though he wanted to come. He waited till she left and then went anyway. He was also in disbelief at how many people John had fooled into thinking he was a good man. He sat in the bushes across the street and watched all the people flock there to put flowers on the ground. He didn't understand it, and he knew John did not deserve this type of condolences. He'd gotten what he'd deserved, and if Ben had had it to do all over, Ben wouldn't have changed a thing. He saw his mom turn and start heading in his direction, so he ran home.

When Amy got home, Ben was sitting on the couch and watching a movie. Amy was exhausted. She walked into the living room, kissed Ben on the forehead, said good night, and went to bed. She wanted to put this day behind her and move on with her life.

Ben waited till he knew his mom was sleeping, and then he tiptoed to the front door. He didn't know why, but he had the urge to go back to John's, and that was exactly what he planned to do. He grabbed his bike, jumped on, and took off down the road. He went to the same place he'd hidden earlier. There were still a couple of people showing up, and there was a cop car sitting out front at his house. As he sat in the bushes, he stared at the house that was all taped off, admiring his work and replaying the vision of stabbing John. He sat there for a few hours, enjoying every minute of it. The people stopped coming, and eventually the cop took off. That was when Ben decided that Mr. Anderson didn't deserve all these flowers. He didn't deserve their attention either, but there wasn't much he could do about that. But the flowers could be destroyed. He looked around to make sure no one was watching, and then he scurried from the bushes to John's front yard. He stood off to the side of the driveway, and he ran out, grabbed some flowers, ran back to the side of the driveway, and ripped them apart. He repeated this till there were no flowers left on the yard. They were now a torn-up mess of nothing strewn across the driveway. When Ben was finished, he added a special touch by defecating on what was left of the mess. Then he took off back home and waited for what was to come. When he got back home, he tried going to sleep, but he was too excited to see the reaction from the people when they discovered what he'd done.

6
CHAPTER

The next morning, Ben came out of his room and went into the kitchen for breakfast. He'd barely slept. All he wanted to do was get on his bike and head over there. It was still early in the morning, and he needed to think of a way to get out of there without raising any suspicion with his mother for wanting to leave so early.

"Mom?" Ben said.

"Yes, dear?" Amy answered.

"Well, you remember all that stuff Mr. Anderson was teaching me about how to stay in shape?"

Amy quivered when he said John's name, but she played it off and answered Ben normally. "Of course. Are you planning on keeping up with it?"

"I think so," Ben answered.

"I think that's a good idea, sweetie. When are you going to start?"

"I want to start running every morning before breakfast," he replied.

Amy thought it was great that Ben wanted to keep up with his exercises, and she encouraged him to do it.

He wanted to be in shape, but this was an excuse to get out of the house this morning. He had no intention of doing it the next day, although he did kind of miss the challenge of it. His plan was to ride his bike, but he thought maybe he would try jogging. He did want to get in shape, and he wanted to be better looking than he was, so maybe it wasn't such a bad idea to keep with it and take what that animal had taught him, using it to his advantage.

He stood up from the table and went to put his shoes on at the front door. He could hear a bunch of voices outside. He opened the door to see the old ladies in the middle of the street again, squawking like birds. It annoyed him for some reason. He hated how they gathered in the middle of the road instead of on the sidewalk. Every time a car came down the road, it would have to honk, and still the ladies would take their sweet time getting off the road. They didn't belong there in the first place. He hoped that someday someone would run them all over, and he hoped he was there to see it. He would think about running up right before they died to laugh and scowl at them for being in the middle of the road. *Like a big "fuck you" before you die.*

Ben stood there and stared at them for a moment until Amy came out to see what the fuss was all about. "What's happening?" she yelled from the doorstep.

The older lady sprung from the group and shouted loudly, "Someone destroyed John's front yard last night!" It was as if she was excited to be the one to say it first. That made Ben even more annoyed. *These old ladies that have nothing better to do than talk about everyone else, as a way of denying their own shitty existence.* "The police are there now, trying to gather more evidence."

Another lady belted out, "Guess someone didn't like him much. Ha!" They snickered a bit and then went silent as they stared down the road, waiting to see what other emergency vehicles would go by.

Ben jogged down the driveway, past the old ladies, and down the street. By the time he reached the end of the street, he was dead tired. He didn't see how he was going to jog all the way over to Mr. Anderson's. On a bike, it was long enough. It would take a half hour on foot. He decided to go for it. He got to the end of the street, took a quick break, and then started up again in the direction the police vehicles were headed. That instantly got the ladies talking. Ben could hear their questions already. "Where'd you go? Why'd you go that way? Did you see anything?" Just thinking about it enraged him. He hoped they weren't there when he came back.

It took him a solid half hour to make it to John's street, and by the time he got there, he was a big sweat bag and could barely breathe. Still, he felt good about making it there. He had never run that much in his life, and all he'd had to do was push himself a little bit. He figured that was the easy part. The hard part was making it back home. He was leaning up against the stop sign at the intersection when he looked down the road and saw all the people standing out in front of the house. A half dozen cop cars were there too. He'd completely forgotten about how tired he was, and like a zombie, he started walking down the street toward the crowd.

As he walked up, he saw men on the front yard picking up the shit he'd left behind and bagging it up. He laughed to himself and got in the crowd. He wanted to hear what people were saying about it. He shuffled his way through the crowd to get to a spot where he could see the house better. He heard a couple of people saying how disgusting this was, and they hoped that the cops caught the killer soon. They were saying stuff like how they would like to get their hands on the guy who did this, or how they thought the killer should be killed in the same way. *All of it is a bunch of tough-guy talk,* Ben thought. He loved being in the crowd, listening to all these people talk about him, the killer—and he was right in front of their faces.

Eventually Ben got bored and decided to head home. There were still lots of people there, so working his way through the crowd was tiring enough for him. He walked to the end of the road and started a light jog down the main street, toward home. The entire way home he thought about how good it had felt to kill Mr. Anderson, and how good it had felt to destroy all the flowers left and then go back the next day to hear everyone gossip about it. It annoyed him that everyone praised Mr. Anderson, but he couldn't come clean. It was too late for that. Justice was served in his eyes.

Before he knew it, he was heading down his street. It was like he was in a trance. He then realized he hadn't stopped once for a break. He had maintained that light jog and hadn't even thought about it. He was quite proud of himself. He got to his front door in a huff and was eager to get some water. He burst into the house and went directly for the kitchen sink to get a glass of water, not even realizing his mother had company. He chugged three big glasses of water and stood at the sink, huffing and puffing.

Ben was startled when he heard April's voice behind him. "Wow, what'd you do? Run a marathon?"

Ben spun around, his eyes wide and full of excitement "Hey, April."

"You started jogging now?" April said as her eyebrows raised, her full attention on Ben's response.

"Yeah. I am going to try to keep up with everything Mr. Anderson taught me."

"Oh, good. That's great, Ben," Kim said. "He would have wanted you to keep up with it. I'm sorry for your loss. I know how much he meant to you."

Ben looked at his mom and back at Kim and smiled. "Yeah, he will be missed," was all Ben could think of. That wasn't completely untrue. He *would* be missed. Just not by any of his victims.

"So, has anyone found out anything about that night? Do they have any suspects or leads?" Amy asked while trying to be nonchalant about it.

Kim knew a few of the volunteers in the fire department, and she always had the lowdown on what was going on in town. "They are completely clueless. They are trying to say this was an isolated incident so none of the residents panic. They don't know what to do."

"Pretty creepy knowing there is a murderer on the loose in our town," April said.

Ben was happy to hear that they didn't have a clue who'd done it.

"Well, whoever it was, I'm sure they had their reason. Hopefully we can all just sleep in peace. If it happens again, then we know we are in trouble," Kim explained.

Ben went to leave the room. He was soaked in sweat from the run, and he didn't want to smell bad in front of April. But before he left, Amy informed him that she was working tonight and April was going to come over. Ben tried hard not to let the excitement show, but he couldn't hold back the extremely noticeable smile that was about to burst out of his face. "Sounds good," he said. Then he headed off to the shower.

Ben could hear them giggle, and he heard Kim say, "I think someone has a crush." He closed the bathroom door behind him. He was embarrassed but got excited at the idea of April knowing how he felt. He thought maybe because she knew, she might make a move on him. He could hope, anyway.

Later that day, when Amy was getting ready for work, Ben sat there eagerly waiting for April to show up. It was the only time he looked forward to not having his mom around. Even when he'd killed John, he couldn't help but wish she could have been there to enjoy it with him.

"There is leftover lasagna from last night that you guys can warm up and have for dinner, okay?" Amy said, walking into the living room while putting on her earrings. "I'll be done at eleven. I expect you to be in bed by the time I get home. You have school tomorrow."

"Yes, Mom," Ben said.

There was a knock at the door, and Ben leapt from the couch and ran to the door. Upon opening the door, he felt all that excitement crash and burn.

"Hey, buddy," April said with a big smile. "This is David."

David reached out his hand for a handshake. He was tall with a strong build. He had dark hair and was very handsome. Ben was instantly pissed off but shook his hand anyway. "Hey, buddy. How are ya?" David said with a big smile.

Ben replied, "Good," and then walked back into the house.

Amy came out of the bedroom, putting her hair up in a ponytail. "Hey, April," she said as she rushed around, picking up the last things she needed before she headed out the door. "You must be David. I'm Amy. Nice to meet you."

David shook her hand. "Nice to meet you too. Your son is in great hands." He gestured to April.

"Oh, I know. She's wonderful. I have to be going though. I'm so late! It was great meeting you, David." Amy headed toward the door. "Love you, Ben. See you tomorrow." She blew him a kiss and left.

Ben couldn't believe that April had a boyfriend and had brought him. He also couldn't believe his mother hadn't even told him about it.

Just then, David dropped down on the couch beside Ben, startling him. "Whoops, didn't mean to scare you, little guy," David said in a condescending tone. He laughed as he grabbed the remote for the TV out of Ben's hand. "My remote now!" David laughed again and started flipping through the channels. He would stop on a show and ask if Ben liked it. Before Ben could reply David, would say, "Too bad," change it, and laugh. He was tormenting Ben for no reason.

Later, David went into the kitchen, where April was getting dinner ready for the three of them. He walked up behind her, wrapped his arms around her waist, and rested his chin on her shoulder. Ben was watching from the couch, and once David noticed that, he grinned and started kissing April's neck.

Ben turned around on the couch and continued watching TV. He picked up the remote and started flipping back to the channel he'd been watching before. Then he heard David yell from the kitchen, "Don't be changing that, bud. I was watching that!"

Ben turned around in anger. "You aren't even watching it. You're in the kitchen!"

David's face filled with anger, and he was about to storm into the living room and take back the remote. However, April grabbed him by the arm and demanded help getting stuff out for dinner. David glared at Ben for a moment and went on helping April in the kitchen. A few minutes later, April called Ben in for dinner. The three of them sat at the kitchen table as April requested. April and David were talking about stuff Ben didn't know anything about. He sat there slowly eating and thinking. He'd wanted to hurt David just for being April's boyfriend, but he'd decided against it. However, after the TV incident, now it was personal. Ben wanted revenge. He wanted to see David cry. He wasn't going to kill him, but he'd hurt him and teach him a lesson. *You can't pick on people just because you are bigger than them.*

When dinner was done, they put their dishes in the sink and retreated into the living room to watch a funny movie April had rented. Ben tried pulling a fast one on David and sat in the middle of the couch to split them up, but as soon as David made it over to the couch, he shoved Ben aside and sat where he wanted. For the rest of the movie, Ben had to sit there listening to the two giggle and whisper to each other. It drove him crazy. He couldn't wait till the movie was over. He sat there stewing in his own hatred for David.

When the movie was finished, April got up to finish the dishes and clean up. It was about eight o'clock, and Ben had another hour before he had to go to bed. He wanted to watch some of the prebedtime shows he always watched. He went for the remote, and as soon as he picked it up, David quickly reached over and grabbed Ben's hand that had the remote, squeezing.

"Listen, you little fuck. You aren't watching more TV. You are going to say you aren't feeling well, and then you are going to go to bed." He threw Ben's hand back at him and turned back toward the TV with the remote. "I'm getting some tonight," David added as he flipped through the channels. He got to a show he liked, looked over at Ben with a shit-eating grin, and said, "I'll kick your ass if you fuck that up for me. Now, get the fuck out of here!"

Ben didn't move from the couch. He sat there and didn't say anything. David started to give Ben little jabs to the side to get him to move, but Ben still sat there, doing his best to ignore the asshole. David was annoyed that Ben didn't move. He looked over his shoulder and saw April had her back to them, doing the dishes. David grabbed Ben by the hair, and before he could make a sound, David brought his other hand to Ben's mouth and nose. David held tight and picked Ben up by the hair. With absolutely no oxygen supply, Ben was powerless. David dragged Ben over to his room and opened the door. Before letting him go, David gave Ben a hard kick in the ass, sending Ben flying to the floor. He waited till Ben turned over on his back, and right before closing the door, Ben heard David laugh and say, "Little bitch. Don't come out of your room tonight, or next time it will be worse."

Ben lay on his floor for another ten minutes before he dragged himself to his bed and pulled himself up. His back was sore from where David had kicked him, and he could hardly move without being in pain. Once he pulled himself up on the bed, he did something he had never done before. His eyes filled with tears, and his bottom jaw started chattering. He closed his eyes, put his hands together, and started praying to God. Ben never really knew what to believe in when it came to religion, but he did believe in God.

He hoped God would answer this prayer, even if it meant never answering another prayer again.

"Dear God. I know I don't deserve an answer or any kind of help from you. I have done some bad things and haven't been the best kid. I pray that you help me change that. I pray that you give me the strength to get through these tough times. I pray that you help me for once. I'm begging you."

When he was done with his prayer, he lay there staring at the ceiling and hoping that something would change. He hoped God would give him a sign tomorrow that everything would be okay. With that thought, he was able to calm down enough to fall asleep.

7
CHAPTER

Ben woke up the next morning pretty sore, but he also had a little glimpse of light at the end of the tunnel. The thought of getting help from God made him feel very positive, and it helped him forget about the beating from the night before. He thought that if there was a God, he would see how fucked up Ben's life was and help in some way.

When he came out of his room, Amy was still sleeping, so he quietly got ready for school and headed out the door. It was a little chilly that morning, and he walked as fast as he could to get to school. He couldn't help but think of the prayer he'd said last night. He was hopeful God would show him a sign, and he kept his eyes peeled the entire walk. As he walked down the street, he talked out loud, saying, "Show me a sign, any sign." He hoped something would pop out.

Just then, he spotted David across the road, biking in his direction. He tried hiding in the hopes of going unnoticed, but within seconds David spotted him. He ramped off the curb and crossed the road. Ben, unsure what to do, stopped in his tracks like a deer caught in the headlights. David pedaled harder and harder, and before Ben knew it, he felt a foot smash into his chest like a jousting pole. He flew off his feet and into the road. A car narrowly missed him as he scurried to catch his footing to get back to the safety of the sidewalk. He looked down the street in David's direction. David pulled over, pointing and laughing with the rest of his buddies. Ben turned around and kept walking in the direction of the school, but instead of going right and crossing the road to school, he turned left and went back home.

When he got home, Amy was just waking up and drinking a coffee at the kitchen table. "What are you doing home?" she asked as she stood up to greet him at the door. As she got closer, she could smell something very bad, like Ben had stepped in dog shit. When she got closer, she realized it was Ben. He had shit himself when he got kicked in the stomach. She saw his clothes were all dirty, and he had a couple of scrapes on his hands and knees. "What happened? Who did this to you?"

Ben lied and said it was a couple of bullies he'd never seen before. Amy cleaned him up and let him do whatever he wanted for the rest of the day.

All Ben wanted to do was sit and watch his favorite TV shows. Amy had to work, and April could only babysit at night, but she figured it would be fine if she left him home. Maybe it would make him feel a bit better to have some privacy. She prepared lunch and dinner for him so that all he had to do was microwave it, and then she started getting ready for work.

Ben lay on the couch watching TV and not saying much. All he could think about was how shitty people were and how he didn't deserve this treatment. Even God couldn't help him, and if God wasn't going to help him, then hopefully he wouldn't help anyone who wronged him, because he was done fighting his urge. *If God doesn't care, why should I?*

It was eleven thirty, and Amy was getting ready to go to work. "I'm leaving now, sweetie." Ben struggled to pull himself off the couch but managed to shuffle over to his mother and give her a hug goodbye. "Food is in the fridge, and the diner's number is on the fridge. Call me if you have any problems." She grabbed Ben by the chin and directed his face at her. "Look at me, sweetie. Don't worry about those other kids. You are a great kid, and I love you." She kissed him on the cheek and gave him a big hug.

"I love you too, Mom."

"There is so much more to life after you are done with school. What happens now won't even matter fifteen years from now."

Amy stood up and headed out the door. Ben sat on the couch and thought about what his mother said. He had a moment where he took everything that had happened to him in at once. He was overwhelmed but concluded that no one in this life would help him. *You are on your own, and only you have the power to change or rearrange things in your life. It's up to you the path you take, the choices you make.* In that moment, he came to the realization that the events that happened today and in his past were the cruel, harsh reality of some people's lives. The signs he was looking for today were quite clear after thinking about it. They were signs that he was on his own and that only he could stand up for himself. No one but him could be his hero. He also realized that he couldn't let David get away with being such a piece of shit.

Ben started thinking about how he was going to get back at David. He thought of ways to kill him and make it look like an accident. He thought about electrocuting him, but he would need to be in his house to make that happen, and Ben didn't like the idea of trying to sneak around a house full of people. He knew David liked to go fishing and thought of possible ways he could try to drown him. That could go south for Ben quick if he lost his footing and slipped into the water.

He thought of a few more things but kept running into the same problems: he either needed to be able to overpower David, which would be a lot harder said than done, or he needed to break into David's house at night, which Ben definitely did not want to do. He thought his best chance to do anything would be at David's fishing spot, and he knew exactly where it was.

He knew David liked to go down there after school. For Ben, it was a ten-minute walk from home. The entrance was a dirt road, and where the dirt road ended was a set of railroad tracks. To the left, the tracks went straight through the north side of town. To the right, about a quarter mile down the tracks, was a railroad bridge called Black Bridge that went for a quarter mile and met the other side of town, which in a car took fifteen minutes to reach. But for those who were brave enough, the bridge took about four minutes to walk across. Below the bridge was a two-hundred-foot drop into a small stream. The stream was where David would to go salmon fishing, and chances were he would be there today after school. To get to there, one needed to walk up to the bridge, and just before it, one took the trail to the left of the tracks and descend down this steep slope of loose dirt and stones. It was a challenge to get up and down, but apparently the fishing was worth it.

Amy was working a double to make up for some time she'd missed, and she wasn't going to be home till eleven at night. Ben had lots of time to follow David around, and he felt it was too soon to do anything yet. He would need to think about it for a bit and then come up with a game plan, like he'd done with Mr. Anderson. He learned from his mother's mistakes: if he acted too quickly, he'd get sloppy. He did not want to be sloppy. He wanted every murder to go off exactly how he'd planned them.

Ben impatiently waited till four in the afternoon and then headed out in some casual hiking clothes and comfortable shoes. It wasn't far, and he didn't want to arrive at the spot at the same time as David did, so he took his time. During his walk there, he couldn't help but keep looking over his shoulder to see if David was sneaking up on him. He started getting nervous, and that nervousness quickly turned to fear the closer he got to the bridge. He didn't realize how scared he was of David. He finally arrived at the part where the road cut off and one either went straight into a heavily wooded area, left back to town, or right toward the bridge. He stood there for a minute, looked down the tracks, and thought about how stupid of an idea this was. If David did see him, there wouldn't be anyone around to hear Ben's scream for help. With every bit of intuition and instinct telling him to turn around and go home, he faced his fear head-on and started down the path toward the bridge.

He was about fifteen feet from the entrance of the trail, so he started to proceed with caution. He wasn't planning on going down the trail; he had intended to go a little way out on the bridge and look down to see if he could see him. He quietly crept past the entrance and slowly edged out on the bridge. He got quite a way out there and could see it was clear that David was not there. It wasn't a complete waste, though. Ben had always been afraid to go out on the bridge, but now that he was out there, he couldn't get over how beautiful the view was. He went a bit farther out and stood there, taking it all in. He wasn't even worried that one misstep would end in absolute death. He actually enjoyed being in the moment—a feeling he was not used to. It almost felt like nothing mattered and all his other worries melted away.

It was all ruined by one short sentence. "Hey, you little fuck!"

Ben knew exactly who it was from the voice, but he refused to look up in hopes that he daydreamed it.

"I'm talking to you," the voice said with a little more anger.

Ben looked up and saw his worst fears materialize in front of his eyes. David stood at the beginning of the bridge. Ben noticed David's bike lying in the grass a few feet away, so Ben knew he wasn't just passing by. David had this evil smile on his face, and without even noticing, every time David took a step forward, Ben took a step back. Before he knew it, he was almost to the middle of the bridge. He had to do something. A few feet more, and the underlay of the bridge stopped; there would be nothing to protect him from falling between the railroad ties.

He decided to stand his ground and tell David off in the hopes that it would get him to back off enough where Ben could get off the bridge. All it did was entice him more. Next thing Ben knew, he was on his belly with David on his back, dragging him closer and closer to the edge. Ben had never been so scared in his life. He thought this was it and David was going to throw him over the side. He screamed and clawed, but it was as if it had no effect on the strength David had. David got Ben to where Ben's head was hanging over the side, and he was forced to look down as David sat on his back, laughing. Ben managed to struggle free, and David couldn't help but laugh so hard that he could barely get up. He laughed even harder when he saw that Ben had pissed his pants. Ben ran off the bridge, and once he got to solid ground, he slowed down a bit, knowing David wasn't going to come after him. He didn't see any point on wasting more energy by running. By the time Ben made it back to the road, David was getting back on his bike. Ben watched as he jumped on his bike and rode it across the tracks like it was no problem. Ben hated the fact that he was impressed by that, but it also gave him a great idea.

There was a tiny, one-person shack on one side of the tracks. It must have been used for anyone working on the bridge who needed somewhere to go if a train came. It was old and sketchy looking, but that was where Ben was going to hide and try to knock David off the bridge. There was no way Ben was going to let him get away with this, and now that he knew for sure that David went there on a daily basis, he could ambush him. The only days he could not go was when his mother wasn't working. Even then, he could still go; he would simply have to lie to his mother, which he did not like doing.

Ben went back a couple of days later when his mother was working, but he was a lot more careful about it. He could not have another experience like he'd had the last time. He got close to the trail, but as he got closer, he could hear voices coming up the trail. He only knew the once voice, but that was enough to make Ben blindly jump into some nearby bushes. As much as it hurt, he bit back a yelp of pain and waited for the two voices to pass. Once he knew the coast was clear, he pulled himself from the thorny bushes and peeked over the shrub to see if they were gone. He saw David and some kid he didn't recognize ride off on their bikes. Ben knew he would be coming back. It was a gamble whether he was coming alone or not, but Ben wanted to test his theory anyway.

He pulled himself from the bushes and carefully headed down the bridge to the tiny little shack off to the side. There were windows on both sides, so he could see anyone coming from either direction. He was there checking stuff out when he noticed David coming back. Ben instinctively ducked down. Then he remembered that this was why he was there after all. He took another peek and saw that David was alone. Ben decided this was the moment of truth. This was when it was going to happen. Once he made up his mind that this was happening, all his fear melted away, and he felt that fight-or-die feeling. He took another look and saw David pedaling down the bridge, closing in quick. Ben crouched down real low and took a deep breath. If he could time it right, he could jump out and slam into David, hopefully sending him flying over the side of the bridge.

All of a sudden, like a cannon ball shooting out of a cannon, Ben came racing out of the door. For a brief moment, he made eye contact with David. In what felt like a minute to Ben, he could see the fear and surprise in David's face, which fueled Ben's rage. Ben hit him so hard that he knocked the wind out of himself. He crashed to the ground with the bike, but he saw David go sailing toward the edge. Ben hit the ground so hard, and the way he landed, he took the handle of the bike right in the sternum, but he knew he couldn't hesitate. He knew that if he didn't knock David over the edge, and David got up first, there would be hell to pay. Ben pulled himself to his feet and saw that David didn't quite go all the way over. He was hanging on to the edge, trying to pull himself up, but he couldn't quite make it. He started calling to Ben for help, and all Ben could do was smile.

Ben darted over there and put out his hand as if he was going to help pull him up. Ben grabbed his hand, and instead of pulling him up, he started pushing it straight out behind David as he struggled to keep a grip with his legs and other arm. David was begging for his life. Ben looked him in the eyes with this dead stare and a creepy grin on his face. He leaned in and said, "God wants you to die!" Then he pushed off David's other hand. Ben watched David fall the entire way, and he still watched after David had hit and was nothing but a bloody mush pile on the rocks below. He could see the red stream of blood flowing down the river. Ben took a couple of minutes to admire his work, and then he got up and left the scene. He did not want to be there when someone discovered David. Even if it did look like a freak accident, he didn't want to take any chances. He made sure nothing of his was left behind and then took off as quickly as he could.

When he got home, he was so fired up and couldn't believe how perfect it had worked out. He loved the fact that David could see who it was and was able to see him enjoy it. That was how he wanted it to go from now on. For the rest of the afternoon, he sat there staring blankly at the TV, daydreaming of killing people. But it was not just killing them—he dreamed of getting close to them while he did it. He thought of different ways to kill people. The only problem was he didn't have anyone who deserved to be killed. He had lots of people he wanted to kill for being shitty, but they weren't shitty enough to kill.

Ben knew there were a lot of shitty people in his town. He remembered when he was younger and his mom and dad were junkies, he would sit at the top of the stairs listening to all of them talk while they got high in the kitchen. It wasn't much, but he was so lonely that he would take what he could get. Sitting there, listening, and watching was enough to get by for him. He would listen to the junkies tell stories of robbing people and stealing from others. He particularly remembered this one man that went by the name of Zippo.

He would always walk about robbing and killing people for fun, for no reason. Ben always got scared when that guy came over. He wasn't ready to go after a guy like that, but he did need someone.

Later that evening, Ben was watching TV with his mom when their program was interrupted with a missing persons report. It was a report on David. Amy gasped at the news because she had met David a couple of times, and she got on the phone with Kim. Ben listened to his mother gossip on the phone, trying to soak up every bit of information she could. Ben loved his mother, but it was clear she was the biggest gossip queen. She was on the phone with Kim for about an hour. Ben stayed in the living room pretending to pay attention to the TV.

Amy walked back into the living room.

"Any news on David?" Ben asked, trying to sound concerned.

"They found him under Black Bridge. Kim said he always fished down there, and he always crossed the bridge. The police are saying he must have fallen over the side when he was crossing," Amy said, still clutching the phone.

"That is too bad. Is April doing okay?"

"She's really hurting. You should call her. She really needs a friend right now." Amy paused for a second, as if she was imagining the feeling of losing a child. "Ugh, his poor parents. I don't even want to imagine what they are going through." Her eyes filled with tears. "Don't ever go playing around on that bridge. When I was a young girl, there were three people I went to school with who accidentally fell over the side. Promise me you won't play around down there." Amy knelt in front of Ben, grabbed him by the hands, and made him promise her.

"I promise. God!" he said with a snarky attitude.

It made him feel like he was being babied, and he didn't like it. He knew his mom was concerned, but he wasn't stupid enough to put himself in danger like that for no reason.

Amy grabbed Ben and hugged and held it for a while. When she let him go, she kissed him on the cheek and took off, dialing a number on the phone.

Ben was proud of his work and even prouder that it had gone according to plan. They were already calling it an accident.

Everything seemed to be going pretty good for Ben. He was still working out as best he could and going on daily jogs. He didn't really think much about killing people; he felt satisfied and didn't have any urge like he'd had the night he killed David.

It was a few weeks later, and everyone had slowly stopped talking about David and the tragic accident. April finally came back to hang out with Ben while Amy went to work. Ben didn't think life would get any better and was almost convinced it was going to be good from here on out. Then one day he came home from school, walked in the door, took off his shoes, and stepped into the kitchen to say hi to his mom—but his mom wasn't alone. There was this tall, dark-haired man with a mustache and glasses. They weren't the geeky kind of glasses, but the kind of glasses that made a man look even manlier.

"Hey, sweetie. How was school?" Amy kindly asked. Ben didn't know what to think, and one could tell by looking at him that he did not like the situation at hand. "Meet Tim. He has a son a few years younger than you."

Ben didn't look impressed by that pointless bit of information. All he wanted to know was who this guy was who was sitting at the kitchen table and why was he there. Ben stood there for a few minutes and went through the whole introduction thing. Then he went to his room to unpack his backpack and start working on his homework, which he milked till dinner to avoid socializing.

He could smell the cooking and followed his nose out to the kitchen, where his mother was preparing his favorite, spaghetti. He sat down at the table and asked about Tim. Amy explained that the man would be around more often because they had started to see each other and really enjoyed each other's company. She reassured Ben that this didn't change anything, and she would always be there for him whenever he needed. That was comforting for Ben to hear, but he still couldn't help but worry that, like the last two guys in his life, Tim would hurt him or his mom. He didn't want to go through that again. She explained to him how happy he made her, and she was going to continue to see him. She reassured him that Tim was a good man and was good for their family. "The first real man in my life," she said to Ben. Ben could see how happy she was and didn't want to ruin it for her, so he figured it'd be best to try to adjust to the new situation.

Everything was going well for the first few months of the new relationship, and for once Ben felt happy. Ben got along with Tim's son, Billy, and Tim treated all three of them really good. Things were finally looking up. He hoped everything would change for the better.

8
CHAPTER

Afew months later, it was getting cold outside, with winter just right around the corner. Ben loved the snow, and every year he would wait with anticipation for the first snowfall of the year. Amy and Ben had watched it every year for as long as he could remember, and they never missed one. It was one of the few good memories he had of his mother growing up.

It was a few days before the first snowfall was going to come, according to the weather station, and Amy and Ben started talking about it at the dinner table one night. Billy piped up and said that he would like to watch it with them too.

Amy thought that was a great idea, but Ben was enraged by it. This was for him and his mom, and thinking about Billy being there made him resentful. He saw this as a threat and started thinking Tim and Billy were driving a wedge between him and his mother; soon it would be just a family of three. Ben felt anxious and started sweating. He had to get up from the dinner table and out of that conversation. The thought of losing his mother to another family haunted Ben. He would die before he let that happen. He did like Tim and Billy, but it wasn't about that anymore. He saw them as a threat now—a threat that he needed to eliminate. He didn't know how, but he wanted them gone, out of his house and out of his life for good. Soon it was all he could think about. All the violent thoughts came rushing back, and the anger entered him like water filling up a balloon. Before he knew it, he was back to thinking about torturing people and had that strong urge to kill someone. He didn't want to upset the balance that was stored in his household; for once his mother was happy and smiling, and he did not want to take that away from her. He thought of so many ways that he could kill Tim and Billy and make it look like an accident, but he didn't want to do that to his mother. He had to direct his anger somewhere else before he did something he would regret.

Later that night, Ben went for a walk to cool down. He needed to clear his head and get away from everyone. He left his front door, went up to the main road, turned right, and kept walking. Before he knew it, he was downtown. This was a milestone for Ben because he had never actually been downtown without his mother, and other than school, he had never been this far from home without his mother. It felt good. He felt like a grown-up, like a man. He walked around for an hour or so, going in and out of the small row of shops on the main drag.

He came out of the last shop as it was getting dark. When he stepped outside, he stood straight up, stuck his nose in the air, and took a deep breath of the crisp, cold, fresh air. He exhaled, leaving a big smile on his face. During his walk, he did a lot of thinking and came to terms with the idea that Billy and Tim would be there whether he liked it or not, and that he needed to get used to it. "I guess it isn't so bad," Ben said aloud. "At least he's not a junkie."

Ben thought it was about time to go home and hang out with his family. As much as Billy annoyed him, he thought it was cool that he now had a little brother. This new accepting nature made Ben feel really good—until he walked past Mr. Anderson's street. It was the street where he'd made his first kill. He wanted to keep walking but couldn't fight this overpowering urge to go down the street.

When he got to the house, there were dead flowers scattered across the front lawn, and the doors still had police tape on them. It was clear Mr. Anderson had no close relatives or friends because no one had come to collect his stuff. Ben was almost mesmerized, standing there and looking up at the house. He started getting flashbacks of the first night he's been there. He saw himself creeping up the side of the driveway and ducking into the backyard.

In the heat of the moment, Ben followed his old footsteps. He ran up the side of the driveway, feeling that same rush, that explosion of serotonin and dopamine filling his brain and body. He ran to the backyard and went up on the back deck. Once he was up there, he started looking through the window, trying to see in. The sun was going down, and it made the inside very shadowy. He looked over at the chair and played it over and over in his head. The urge to kill was so strong now.

He stayed there for a few more minutes and then took off home. If he was gone too long, his mother would worry, and he didn't want that. He got back on the main street that he lived off and started jogging. He was about halfway home when a man who looked familiar to him was out on his front lawn as Ben jogged by. The man started laughing and yelled out, "Keep jogging, fat boy." Then he laughed some more and went about his business. While the man went about the rest of his day without a second thought about the exchange, Ben was furious. He jogged back home with nothing but rage and curiosity driving him. He got home and burst through the door, startling Amy, Tim, and Billy. Ben was so mad that his eyes had filled with tears on the jog, and they'd frozen to his face.

Amy noticed this and ran over to him. "What happened? Baby, what happened?"

Ben took off his boots and coat. He didn't want Tim and Billy to see him cry, so he wiped away the frozen tears, choked back the massive lump in his throat, and got to the point where he was able to say some words without bursting into tears. "Some guy called me fat when I was jogging just now."

Amy jumped up like a mother lioness who'd just seen her cub being stalked by a hyena. She got good at controlling her anger, but when it came to her kid, she had a hard time thinking rationally. Tim saw Amy go into death mode, and he quickly went over to talk her down. He didn't know much about her past, but he did know she had a bad temper, and he didn't want that side coming out because of some jackass with a big mouth.

"Where does he live? Does he live on this street? Is it that fat piece of shit who lives two doors down?" Amy had a pulsating vein on her forehead that flared with every word.

Tim gently put his hands on her shoulders from behind and eased her into him. He slowly rubbed his hands up and down her arms. "Are you okay, buddy?" Tim asked as he looked over at Ben.

"Yeah, I'll be fine. It's all right, Mom. If you go there, you will kill him and go to jail."

Amy was still enraged till she heard something that completely snapped her out of her rage mode. As Ben walked past her, he whispered only loud enough for her to faintly hear him, "But I won't." Then he headed off to his room. Amy stood there for a minute wondering if what she'd just heard was in her head or if her son had actually said that.

Later, Ben walked out of his bedroom and into the living room to join Billy. Amy was watching Ben from the door, and right before Ben sat on the couch, he looked up and smiled at Amy, but it wasn't a regular smile. It was a smile that one would only hear about in scary stories, a smile that would scare even the mother who'd birthed him. It was a smile through the devil's teeth. He sat down on the couch, and Amy joined Tim in the kitchen.

Tim was pouring a cup of coffee. "You okay?" he asked as he blew on the coffee before taking a sip.

"Yeah, I'm fine. He's just been through a lot, and sometimes I overreact."

"Hey, I can't blame you. I would do anything for my son's happiness. Do you want me to talk to him? Tell him how shitty people can be?" Tim chuckled, trying to make light of the situation.

Amy laughed. "Maybe not in those words."

Tim kissed Amy on the forehead and went into the living room to watch TV with the boys. Amy sat down at the kitchen table with her coffee, watching the three of them laughing and watching TV together. She couldn't ignore what Ben had said, and she had an instinctive urge to do a little investigating herself.

Later that night, Ben and Billy were getting ready for bed. It was such a small place, so when Tim and Billy stayed over, Billy had to sleep in Ben's room. Ben didn't mind. He hated the dark and found comfort with Billy sleeping in his room. Billy was in the bathroom, and Ben was in the bedroom making his bed.

Tim walked in. "Hey, buddy. Can I talk to you for a minute?"

"Yeah, come in," Ben replied.

Tim sat on the bed beside him. "You okay?" Tim asked.

"Yeah. Why wouldn't I be?" Ben snapped back.

"Well, you seemed pretty upset when you got home today."

Ben put his head down and didn't say anything, as if he was embarrassed of what had happened or that he was busted for crying. Either way, he couldn't find any words to say.

"You know what people used to call me in school?" Tim continued.

Ben looked up with curiosity. "You used to get teased?"

"All the time. I used to get called four eyes, and I got stuffed into my locker all the time. It sucked."

"How did you get them back?" Ben asked.

"I got back at them by living well. Till my divorce, of course, and then I was living in hell." Tim laughed. "I'm just kidding. My point is you can't let what people say get you down, because at the end of the day, their opinions don't really matter. When you are done with school, you will leave and never look back, and you will have a great life. They say the best revenge is to live well. So live well. Keep doing what you are doing. All right?"

"All right," Ben answered.

"Good. Now, get some sleep. Good night, buddy," Tim said before he gave Ben a pat on the shoulder and left the room. A few minutes later, Billy came in and got into the bed that was made up for him on the floor. Billy said good night, but Ben lay there silent. He wasn't sure how to take what Tim had said, and he was very conflicted. On one hand, he loved his mom and wanted her to be happy. With Tim, she did seem happy. But on the other hand, how could he trust any male figure who came into their lives now? He really wanted to believe that Tim was a good man, but any trust he had left in him after his father had gone out the window when Mr. Anderson did what he did. Ben lay awake for a while that night, contemplating everything until he finally fell asleep.

The next morning, they all woke and had a big family breakfast together. Ben was still conflicted about the idea of them being there, but he was even more pissed off about the night before when the neighbor had called him fat. Today he was going to do some recon to see if the man deserved to die. When they were done eating, Ben went out for a jog toward the man's house. When he got to the house, he made a quick pass but didn't see anyone outside or any movement inside. There was only one vehicle in the driveway, and it seemed like the man lived there by himself. It was particularly cold that morning, and there was no way Ben was going to stay out any longer than he had to. He thought it would be better to come back in the night. Ben found it was easier to see in people's houses at night when they had their lights on. He went another block before he turned around and headed back home.

For the rest of the day, Ben spent his time hanging out with his family. He was still a bit leery and thought it was a matter of time before something went wrong. It was a weird feeling for him because he'd never felt what it was like to be a part of a real family where everyone cared for each other.

Later that night, he went out for another jog. Amy loved the idea of him jogging but was a little suspicious that he was going twice. She had a feeling he was up to something, so she followed him. She told Tim she was running to the store and followed Ben far enough behind him, so he didn't suspect a thing. She followed him and found it hard to keep up. When Ben stopped in front of a house, she was relieved. She could barely focus on anything besides catching her breath while she hid behind a set of bushes. Then she saw why they had stopped. She stood there in the dark behind some bushes and watched Ben hiding behind a shrub, monitoring a house and writing stuff down on a notepad. He stayed there for a good fifteen minutes before he closed his book. Amy saw that he was coming, so she sprinted back home. She wanted to beat him, so he didn't find out she had left at the same time as him. She knew Ben was slow, but she also knew he was very observant and would instantly become suspicious.

By the time Ben made it back home, Amy had already been home for a few minutes and was already in the shower. Ben came in the house, went straight into his room, and stashed his book under his mattress. Then he went out to the living room and watched TV with Tim and Billy.

The next morning, they woke up to do their regular routine. The kids got ready for school while the adults got ready for work. Ben and Billy went to different schools, so Tim would take Billy. Amy walked Ben to school and then headed to work. This morning was different, though. Everything was regular till Amy dropped Ben off at school. Instead of going to work like she normally would, she went back home. While she walked home, she decided to walk past the house Ben had visited the other night. She wanted to see it in the daytime. As she came up to it, she saw an old man sitting on the porch of an old house. As she walked closer, she noticed that he was watching every step she took. Once she was right in front of the house, she confronted the man about calling her son fat. The man laughed and went into his home. Amy was enraged and walked up to the door, but she was stopped in her tracks when the man reopened the door holding back a vicious German shepherd.

"One more step, and you are lunch," the man said, laughing like a crazy person. Amy had had a fear of dogs ever since she'd been a little girl and had been attacked by a random mutt roaming the streets.

She was so terrified that she turned and ran, and she didn't stop still she got home. Once she was inside, she slammed the door shut behind her and leaned against it as if she was trying to keep the door from falling. For a minute, she completely forgot why she'd gone there, but she snapped back to reality and remembered she had some investigating to do. That clearly was the guy she thought, but she needed to find Ben's notepad. She knew that it had the answers, and answers were exactly what she was seeking.

When she was able to calm down a bit and stop hyperventilating, she took off her outdoor clothes and headed into Ben's room. It took her two minutes before she found his notebook. When she opened it to the first page, she was mortified. She couldn't believe what she was looking at. It was a full page of information on the guy that called him fat.

> 24 Vincent Road
> Old man, 5'8", lives alone. Fenced-in yard; back door is always
> unlocked. Goes to bed at 9:00 p.m. and is up by 6:00 a.m. Sleeps
> in the far left corner of the house. Is outside all day doing nothing.
> Has a dog.

She flipped to the next page and saw words, but they were scribbled out to the point where the paper was torn. After looking closer, she saw that the one word was Mr. and the word beside it started with an A. It took her a few moments to put it together, but once she did, she felt so sick to her stomach. She felt she needed to do something and thought the best course of action would be to confront Ben about it. She didn't believe there was any way Ben was the one who'd killed John. John was such a big man that there wouldn't be any way Ben could come close to him with a knife.

She left his room without looking around anymore. She set the book down at the kitchen table and she left it sitting there till Ben came home from school later that day. When he got home, Amy was sitting at the kitchen table.

"Hey, Mom," Ben said when he saw her sitting at the table. Then he noticed the notebook sitting next to her. Ben's mood completely changed from happy to mad. He looked at his mother with this evil look. "Why do you have that?" he demanded.

Amy sat up straight in the chair. She tried being the alpha in the situation and puffed out her chest. She said in a very angry and aggressive, "Why do you have that?" She stabbed a finger into the book with force. He knew there was no explaining himself out of this one, so he stood there silently

This was very frustrating for Amy. After the yelling didn't work, she stood up, grabbed Ben by the hair, and dragged him toward his bedroom. There were only a few seconds of this Ben could handle. Without even thinking about it, he grabbed Amy's arm and twisted it. She let go instantly, and Ben grabbed his notebook and ran out the door. She'd never felt Ben's strength before, but when he grabbed her arm and twisted so effortlessly, she'd heard and felt a couple of pops. She realized that Ben wasn't just a kid anymore and he was much stronger than she'd thought.

She sat down at the kitchen table, clutching her wrist. She knew it wasn't broken, but it hurt a lot. As she sat there, she debated calling the police. She knew Ben wasn't right, and she knew he was going to do something to that old man. If she didn't stop it, the blood would be on her hands—but at the cost of losing her son. She was pretty sure her son was the way he was because of her.

Later that night, when Ben came home, Amy was drinking a coffee at the kitchen table. "Where were you, Ben?" she said in a low but stern voice.

Ben looked at her like a deer caught in the headlights. "I went for a walk," Ben said, and then he started walking toward his bedroom.

Amy was afraid to push it any further. She wasn't afraid he was going to attack her for confronting him. She wasn't afraid of him lying. She was afraid he would be completely honest and tell her exactly what had happened, and her worst nightmare would be realized.

Ben went to his room, where he stayed for the rest of the night.

The next morning, they both woke up and did their regular routine. The first thing Amy did when she got up was turn on the radio to see if there was any news about last night. She was worried Ben had gone out and done something bad, and she figured if he had, it would be on the morning news. Much to her shock, there was nothing. She looked outside to see if the ladies were gathered at the road. Nothing. *Maybe he didn't do anything*, she thought. With that thought, she was able to start her day in a happy mood.

Ben came out and sat at the table. Amy instantly apologized for how she'd acted, and she told him that if he ever needed to talk about something, he could go to her. He could trust her with anything, and she would never do anything to hurt him. Ben felt very comforted by this and decided that his secrets might be too much for her to handle. He apologized for twisting her arm, and they both put it in the past.

Amy walked Ben to school and then headed to work. She decided to take the long way to work and pass by the old man's place, just to put her mind at ease. It wasn't far, so she was there in no time. When she got to the road and looked in the direction of his house, she didn't see a bunch of cop cars or a crowd of people. She felt relieved. Instead of going further and investigating the house, she decided to not walk down there in case he was out front again, like last time. She didn't want to have another altercation with him or his dog, so she kept walking to work. She was done at four, and Ben would be home from school around three thirty.

When she got home, Ben was sitting on the couch watching the local news channel, which Amy found very strange because she never had seen him watch the news before. It gave her a bad feeling.

"Hey, Ben," she said as she took off her shoes.

Ben was so focused on the news that he completely ignored his mother. He sat there on the edge of the couch as if he was waiting for something to come on. All Amy could do was watch him. He looked so different sitting there. She barely recognized him. It was him, but he looked possessed, like a little monster.

Maybe it was because she was so focused on him, or her eyes were playing tricks on her, but in an instant, Ben snapped his head toward her so fast that Amy didn't have time to react. For a few brief moments, they made eye contact, and what she saw was not her son. When she looked into his eyes, she saw emptiness and blackness. It was the most terrifying feeling a mother could experience—especially because she was the cause.

They stared at each other for a few moments until Amy walked back into the kitchen. She stood at the sink and looked out the window, tears filling her eyes as she clutched at the dishrag in the sink. She tried hard not to cry. She took ten deep breaths and slowly opened her eyes as she exhaled her last breath. She spun around from the sink to look in the fridge, but she was caught off guard when she turned and Ben was right there. It startled Amy so much that she jumped back and smashed her back on the edge of the countertop. She cried out in pain and fell to the floor.

"What the fuck are you doing right there, Ben?"

Ben went to his knees beside her. "I'm sorry, Mom. I didn't mean to scare you. Are you okay?"

Amy grabbed Ben's hand with one hand and grabbed the counter with the other. Together they were able to get her to her feet, but she was still in quite a bit of pain. Ben helped her to the couch and laid her down. *He's so gentle,* Amy thought. She couldn't believe that he would hurt someone. But she also couldn't believe he would have a book of violence either.

Ben grabbed a couple of pillows from his room and put them under her feet and legs. "Don't worry about dinner, Mom. I'll make grilled cheese and soup for us. Sound good?"

Amy smiled. "Yes, sweetie. That sounds great."

She watched him as he started getting dinner ready. She didn't notice a hint of whatever it was she'd seen sitting on the couch just moments ago. He was completely fine. He was acting normal and being himself. She started thinking about what had just happened. Why was he standing so close to her? Why did he sneak up like that? What if she hadn't turned around when she did?

These questions started rattling around in her brain, which made her afraid to take her eyes off her son. It was not for just her safety but for another person's safety too. She didn't know what to do, but she did know she didn't want to spend the night alone there with him tonight.

"Ben, can you bring me the phone, please?"

It was silent in the kitchen for a moment. "What for?"

"I want to call Tim," Amy said.

"What? Am I not good enough to take care of my own mother?"

"No, Ben. I just want to talk to him. Can you please bring be the phone? Now!"

Ben grabbed the phone and stomped his way over to his mother. "Here!" He slammed the phone in her hand so hard that she thought for a second he'd broken something, but she didn't want to let on that it hurt, so she bit her tongue and snatched it from him. She still had control over him as his mother, but how long would that last?

She called Tim and told him what was going on, and she called work and said she wouldn't be coming in for her shift in the morning.

Ben continued to cook dinner, and when she was off the phone, he instantly asked her if Tom and Billy were coming over. Amy was sore and didn't want to fight, so she said no and didn't elaborate at all. That seemed to make Ben happy, and he continued getting dinner prepared for his mother. They ate dinner while watching TV, and when they were done Ben cleaned up everything.

After Ben was done doing the dishes, he went off into his room. A few moments later, he came back out in his jogging shorts and running shoes.

"Going for a run?" Amy asked.

"Yeah, just a short one. I won't be long," Ben said. Then he headed out the door before his mother could hold him up any longer. Ben went outside, took a deep breath in, jumped off the front steps, and headed down the street. His only objective was to see if they'd found that old man yet. It bothered him that they hadn't. He wanted to watch it on the news, and he wanted to come down to the scene of the crime with everyone. He started regretting killing the man inside. It was like an itch that wasn't itched till he saw the ending of it. It was like closure for him, so he could move on to the next victim.

As he came upon the old man's house, he saw there was still nothing going on. This was very frustrating for him, and he started getting angry. He picked up a giant rock and threw it through the big front window, and then he turned around and ran like hell. It was almost dark out, so he hoped that if anyone did see him, they wouldn't have made out his face. He ran all the way home like someone was chasing him and let up once he got to his driveway.

When he came through the door, his mother was lying on the couch and watching TV. "Back already?" she asked.

"I didn't want to be gone long, in case you needed something," Ben said as he walked past her and headed into his bedroom. He came out with shorts and a T-shirt and slumped on the couch at Amy's feet.

Amy noticed something was wrong and asked Ben about it, but all he said was he was tired, and then he got up and went to bed. She knew it was something more than that. Whatever it was, she knew it couldn't be good. He had that same look in his eyes from earlier that day, and she wanted nothing more than for him to be in his room away from her.

Ben lay in his bed all night thinking about the old man and how no one had found him yet. The anticipation was killing him, and he wanted it to be over.

When he got up in the morning, he went to have a shower and saw Amy was still sleeping on the couch, so he tried to be quiet. She was woken soon after Ben got in the shower by the sound of sirens flying by her street. She lay there a minute, listened as the sirens went by, and got a gut-wrenching feeling. She noticed the sirens weren't fading off in the distance like usual. They were close. Close enough that when she turned and looked out the window, she could see flashing lights on one of the buildings a couple of blocks down.

Ben walked out of the bathroom and looked out the window with Amy. "What do you think happened, Ben?" Amy said, almost in a judging tone.

Ben picked up on it and went from a grin to a full-out smile from ear to ear. "How would I know?" He focused his attention back on the window. He wanted to see if those nosy old ladies were out, and sure enough, they walked out of their houses one by one and met in the middle of the street. Ben wanted to get a closer look, so he went over to the door and grabbed his shoes.

Before he could get out the door, Amy started questioning him. "Where are you going?" she demanded.

Ben stood up after putting on his shoes. "I'm going to check it out." Then he left and shut the door behind him before Amy could say anything else. She tried getting off the couch but was in too much pain and gave up. She turned the TV to the news, and there was a live broadcast on the local news channel. Amy wasn't shocked when she saw it was the old man's house. She wanted to give her son the benefit of the doubt, and she wanted to hear the cause of death before she jumped to any conclusions. They were about to do an interview with the chief of police, who was going to give a statement on the situation.

The news channel was waiting for their interview, and in the meantime they had the camera's live feed: a shot of the house with the crowd in it. Amy was watching when she noticed Ben in the background. He was in the crowd of people watching what was happening. Ben was more at the back of the crowd by the police cars when the dog pound arrived to remove the shepherd from the room in which it was locked. On their way out, they had the dog on a leash and were walking past the crowd of people. When they got down to where Ben stood, the dog snapped, barking and growling at Ben. But no mind was paid to it, and they dragged it off. Amy saw it all on the live feed and instantly knew her son was the reason that man was dead.

The chief of police came on about twenty minutes later, and all he said was there was a fatal accident but foul play was not suspected. Amy still didn't believe it. She knew Ben was involved somehow, and she was going to ask him when he got home.

9
CHAPTER

Ben went for a run after he left the scene. He was pumped up and couldn't go home yet. It was about a half hour later when Ben came through the door. He found his mother waiting by the front door for him. "What the fuck did you do, Ben?"

"I didn't do anything," Ben said with a shrug.

"I saw you on TV! I know you were there!"

It wasn't until Amy mentioned he was on TV that he turned around and started listening to her. The thought of being on TV so everyone could see him appealed to him.

They still hadn't released the grim details of what had happened, which was disappointing to Ben, but he knew it would come out sooner than later. He never expected to hear what happened in the days the man was left there, dead.

When the police report came out, it claimed he had died from electrocution in the bathtub. Apparently when he was taking a bath, the radio he had set up had fallen in the tub with him. But what was even more disturbing was the fact that the dog had eaten most of the man's upper half, and as a result they weren't able to do a full autopsy. Ben hadn't expected that, but he thought it was awesome that it had happened—a bonus to his work.

Later that day, Amy was sitting in the kitchen and drinking a coffee. She stared off into nothing. Her concentration broke when she noticed Ben standing off to the side, looking at her. "What is it, Ben? Why are you standing there and staring at me?"

"I did it, Mom!"

Amy looked at Ben with a very confused look on her face. "Did what, Ben?"

"I killed them. It wasn't an accident. I killed them and made it look like that."

Amy didn't know what to say. It wasn't a hard sell; she instantly believed him. All her suspicions had just come true. Her worst fear manifested in front of her. She knew Ben was too far gone, but she loved him. It was her son, and she blamed herself for Ben's actions.

For a few minutes, she sat there in silence, not knowing what to say. Ben stood there waiting for a reaction. The only thing that Amy could get out was to ask why, and Ben's answer was more horrifying than the thought of him killing people. "I like the feeling of taking a life," he said nonchalantly. Amy's jaw hit the floor. She'd created a monster, and there was nothing she could do about it. He was too far gone. The only thing she could do now was either turn him in to prevent him from killing more people or find a way to keep him somewhere where he couldn't hurt anyone else.

Amy started crying. "I'm so sorry, Ben. I'm so sorry. I made you like this."

Ben stood there with no emotion on his face, no look of remorse. He quietly watched his mother crying. "You didn't make me like this. I was born to hurt people who hurt other people. I do it because they deserve it."

Seeing Ben justify it like that reassured Amy that he wasn't going to change. This was now a part of him. He was never going to lose it, and it would always be there to haunt and hurt people. It wasn't like he was out killing bad guys like some sort of superhero. No, he was out hurting people who hurt him, and he believed what he was doing was okay. Amy had to do something. She didn't want to lose her only boy, but she couldn't let him outside knowing he had killed people. She had to think of a way to keep him inside until she figured out something to do with him.

Ben walked over to his mother, who was now sitting on the kitchen floor and leaning against the cupboards. She stared at the ground in disbelief. Ben gently placed his hand on his mother's shoulder. "I would never hurt you, Mom." Then he turned around and walked into the living room, where he started watching TV. Amy couldn't believe what she was seeing. Her son had just admitted to killing people and said they deserved it, and now he was sitting on the couch and laughing at a TV show. It scared the shit out of her. She couldn't move. All she could do was sit there in crippling fear as she watched her murderous son laughing at a show. She'd never sleep again. She could never turn her back on him. Who knew what he was capable of?

As Amy sat on the floor, she came out of her state of shock. She started thinking about what Ben had actually said. "I killed them," he'd said. Them? She thought. She had a suspicion of John but had lost it when it was deemed an accident. But who was the third? She thought about it for a minute, and then it hit her. She knew who the other person was: David, April's boyfriend.

Amy sat there for a few hours, not knowing what to do. She tried coming up with a plan, but nothing worked. Any scenario she came up with in her head ended with Ben overpowering her and making things worse. She needed help. She needed someone she trusted enough to tell this stuff to, but someone who wouldn't call the cops and turn in Ben even though that was exactly what he deserved. She had no choice but to ask Tim. He was a good man, but he knew how strong a parent's love was. Ben might be a killer, but Amy still loved him. He was her son, and she would love him unconditionally. She thought that if she and Tim could restrain him, she could talk some sense into him or try to reprogram his way of thinking. She was his son and even though he might be too far gone, she had to try. She had to try to fix him. After all, she knew it was her fault he was life this and she blamed herself over anyone. Even Ben.

She had a basement where they could keep him, but it was a matter of getting him down there and maybe chaining him to something, so he couldn't escape. She thought that if she could have time with him where she was in control, she would be able to fix him. She didn't want to give up just yet.

After coming up with a plan, she felt a bit better about everything and was able to pull herself up from the floor. She wanted to instantly put these plans in motion before he had time to leave again, but she needed to do it in a way where he wouldn't suspect a thing. The first thing she needed to do was get Tim on board. She had no idea how this would go. She was taking a chance with this plan, but she knew she couldn't do this herself, and due to her history of drug abuse, she'd lost every friend she'd had who she could trust. At that moment, she had never felt so alone and helpless.

She went into the other room and called Tim, asking him to meet at the diner that afternoon. He could tell there was an unsettling urgency in her voice, so he prepared for the worst, which in his head was her breaking up with him.

When Amy got off the phone, she walked up beside Ben, who was still watching TV. She placed her hand on his head and started running her fingers through his hair. She couldn't help but cry. She kept thinking about how this was her baby, and she'd ruined him. She'd killed the little boy inside of him and grown a monster. She turned around before she started crying hard enough that he would notice, and she got changed before she met up with Tim.

She was in her room putting on her pants when she could feel someone staring at her. She could feel it so much that it felt like there were holes being burned into her body. She turned around and saw Ben standing in the doorway with an angry look on his face. "Where are you going?" he asked.

"I have to run into work for a few minutes. I won't be long at all."

Ben stood there for a few seconds and then turned around and went back to watching TV on the couch.

Amy was creeped out, but for some reason she didn't fear him. She knew deep down that Ben would never lay a finger on her. She continued to get ready and gave Ben a kiss on the cheek before she left.

When she walked up to the diner, she noticed Tim's vehicle was parked there, and she went inside. Tim was off in the far corner booth by himself, staring out the window. When she walked up to the table, Tim stood up and gave her a kiss on the cheek. Upon pulling away, he could instantly tell something was very wrong. They sat down at the table, sitting across from each other. She told him everything. She had intended to hold some stuff back, like her killing her husband, but she didn't. She let everything out.

Tim, as an outsider looking in, reassured Amy's suspicion. Tim suggested calling the police but instantly retracted his statement because incriminating Ben would incriminate Amy. Either it was Tim's love for Amy or he actually felt this way, but he seemed to agree with Amy on everything. He even said she was in the right with killing her husband. He simply wished Ben didn't have to be a part of it.

Telling Tim made it feel like a weight had been lifted from her shoulders. But there was still the problem of figuring out what to do with Ben. Tom did not feel comfortable letting Ben play with his son anymore, and Amy understood that. In fact, she felt more comfortable that way too.

They sat there for a little while, trying to come up with a game plan, but she didn't want to be gone from home too long so as to not raise Ben's suspicion. They decided they were going to give it the night to think about and decide what to do tomorrow. They would head back to their homes and meet back at the diner tomorrow at noon.

Amy felt good about this. She was happy she'd told Tim. She felt like she wasn't the only one carrying this burden anymore. She had some help, a leg to stand on. She felt good that she might actually be able to help her son, and that she didn't have to turn her or her son into the police. She didn't regret killing her husband, but she did regret how it had happened. She felt what she'd done had to be done, and she couldn't do jail time for it. That wasn't even an option. She had to fix her son or move to the Canadian Rocky Mountains, where there was nobody around. It would suck for sure, but she would rather do that than spend the rest of her life in jail.

The entire walk home, she thought about ways to gain full control over Ben. If she could do that, maybe she could alter his mind. She thought about drugging his food, and when he passed out, they could carry him downstairs, where they would have an easier time finding a way to restrain him.

She had sleeping pills she could use, but she wasn't sure how much to give him. The thought of drugging her son made her sick, but she had no choice. She finally got home, and when she walked through the front door, she noticed Ben wasn't on the couch watching TV. She looked in his bedroom, but he wasn't there. She went outside in the backyard and the front yard. He was nowhere to be found. She started to panic, standing at the end of the driveway and looking down the street both ways. She thought he might have gone for a jog, and she was overreacting. She turned around and went back inside. Wherever he was, he would be home sooner than later, so she watched some TV until she had to start prepping dinner.

It didn't take long before she had fallen asleep on the couch. A few hours later, she woke up to a song playing on the TV. The sun was starting to go down, and Ben still wasn't home. This was very odd for Ben to be gone this long. But what could she do besides patiently wait? He was a big enough kid that the chances of someone trying to kidnap him were slim. She knew he was okay, but that was not what worried her. What worried her was what he might be doing. She couldn't bear the news of another "accidental death" when she knew damn well it was her son.

It was around eight o'clock when Ben finally got home. Amy was pacing back and forth in the house. She went from worried to mad. As soon as he walked in the door, she was all over him like white on rice. It was like an interrogation. For the first time in a long time, Amy wasn't afraid of Ben—Ben was afraid of Amy. In the midst of her yelling and screaming, Ben broke down and started crying. The moment that happened, she saw the little boy in him, that innocent, beautiful boy of hers, and that made her cry too. She decided to take a different approach. She decided to talk to him and see if she could get some answers from him.

By now they were both sitting on the floor. Amy cradled Ben in her arms, rocking back and forth. Ben's arms were wrapped tightly around Amy's waist. It was a nice moment for them—a moment that Amy saw as an opening.

"Did you hurt someone else tonight?" she lightly whispered in Ben's ear.

Ben didn't say anything, but he nodded yes. Amy bit her lip, tightened her grip around Ben's head, and let out a small gasp that kept her from crying.

"Did the person hurt you?" Amy was hesitant with that question because she feared the answer. She could see hurting someone who hurt him, but she couldn't forgive hurting innocent people.

Ben didn't respond. She slightly adjusted him to sink in a deeper hug. "Who was it?" she asked.

Ben still didn't say anything. Amy pulled his head back from where he rested and looked deep into his eyes.

"Why are you doing this? What is going through your head that tells you to hurt people?"

"I enjoy watching people die," Ben said while staring his mother in the eye.

Amy grabbed Ben by the face with both hands. "Who did you kill this time, Ben? Who was it?"

Ben coldly replied, "Even if I told you, what would you do? I believe what I am doing is right. Just like when you killed dad because you thought it was right."

Amy sat back against the cupboards while Ben pulled himself up from the ground. "You want to know who I killed and how? Watch the news." Then he walked over to the couch, sat down, and started watching the news channel.

Amy stayed sitting on the floor and leaning against the cupboards. She thought about her options while dreading the moment the news came on about another dead person found in town. The ten o'clock news hadn't been on yet, and she sat there waiting. She looked at the clock: it was ten minutes to ten. She pulled herself up and walked over to the kitchen sink to get a glass of water. She stood there sipping on the water and looking out the window, in the opposite direction of the TV set. She could still hear it; Ben made sure of that. It made her sick to her stomach, seeing him waiting for the news to come on. But what was even worse was his certainty that it would be on the news so fast. Whatever he'd done, it must have been in public and must have been very noticeable.

A couple of minutes went by, and a commercial came on for the news stating they had some breaking news that would shock the town. Amy cringed at that. She heard Ben whisper a celebratory, "Yes," when they mentioned breaking news. A few more commercials, and the news was going to be on. Amy stood there, shaking and stunned. She had a feeling that this was going to prove what kind of monster he really was. By now he was no longer sitting on the couch. He was standing up, waiting with anticipation.

Ten o'clock hit. The breaking news came on. It was what she feared—and more.

There was an old bakery that had been in the town for many years. The couple who operated it was well into their seventies but worked liked they were in their twenties. Everyone in town went to this bakery, and everyone knew the old couple as if they were family. The news showed a bunch of emergency vehicles out front of the bakery, and there was a shot of someone being rolled out in a body bag. The old man stood off to the side, crying and breaking down. The camera caught this, and Ben let out a laugh. They still hadn't said what had happened, but the chief of police was going to make his statement soon, according to the news anchor.

Amy still hadn't turned around to look at the screen, but she could see Ben's reflection in the window. He was watching the news like one watched a hockey game. He kept whispering, "Get to how she died, get to how she died," as if he was proud of what he'd done. There was about ten more minutes of the camera taking shots of the crowd. Ben stood there watching, smiling, and admiring his work.

The news anchor came back on to notify the people watching that the chief was making his speech now, and lots of questions would be answered.

The chief came on and said everything but what the people wanted to know. He was extremely vague and uninformative. All he was able to say was that she'd had a work accident, and that her husband was out of the shop at the time. When he returned, it was too late. There was nothing he could do besides turn off the machine.

Ben wasn't happy with this lack of information. He started flipping through the channels, looking for other news coverage on it, but of course there was nothing. He tossed the remote to the couch and ran off to his room. Amy grabbed the phone and called her friend who usually had the lowdown on everything that happened in town. The line was busy for a solid hour, but Amy finally managed to get through and find out what was going on. She was horrified by what she learned.

The husband left to go get more flour from the grocery store. The wife stayed back and prepared the massive spiral mixer with all the remaining ingredients. It was an industrial-size one they'd had in operation. They were the only bakery for miles, and they did everything from bread to cakes. The husband said that something went horribly wrong in the ten minutes he was gone because he walked in the back of the store and didn't see his wife anywhere. All he could here was a mild *thump* sound every few seconds. He didn't know where it was coming from until he saw the mixer was on. When he saw that, he thought his wife couldn't be far, so he grabbed the flour and went to dump it in the mixer. That was when he realized his wife was being mixed in with the batch. He shut it down as quickly as possible, ran over, and tried pulling her out. There was still a little bit of life left in her because she reached up and grabbed at him as one last desperate attempt to cling to life. But she was snagged on something, and he couldn't find out what it was.

When the police got there, they drained the mixer and realized the apron she was wearing got tangled up in the mixer. It had pulled her in before she'd had time to react. They ruled it as a workplace accident.

The next day, Amy left to meet up with Tim at the diner. She was completely convinced that restraining Ben in the basement was not only her best option but also her only option. She needed to convince Tim of the same thing, and after last night, she didn't see that being very difficult. When she walked up to the diner, she saw he was there and again in the back corner of the diner. She slid into the seat in front of him. Amy noticed Tim seemed kind of nervous. Besides the odd joint here and there, Tim was a pretty straight-edge guy. He had never been in trouble with the law, and he always thought stuff through.

When Tim went home yesterday, Ben was all he could think about. In the spur of the moment, he was all for helping and doing what he could. But when he got home and thought about it more, he thought about his life and his son's life, which was most important to him. He was all his son had and he couldn't jeopardize that. Amy had to sit there and listen to all of Tim's concerns, and she agreed with every one of them. She didn't want to put him in that situation, and she realized that going to him was selfish. She should never had done it in the first place. She told him exactly what she planned to do and stated she wanted him there more for the emotional support than the actual physical support, although it would help.

Tim scratched his head in frustration. He took a long, deep breath and exhaled. Then he suggested that he go to the cops and simply not say anything about her killing her husband. Amy explained to him that even if she did go to the police, there was no proof her son was involved in any of it. The murders had been ruled accidents. She had nothing to go on. After she made this clear to Tim, he agreed to help move Ben to the basement, but that was it. He explained to her that what she wanted to do would be considered kidnapping and unlawful imprisonment of someone. Those were big charges, and they would certainly mean jail time. He couldn't take that risk, but he agreed to help her get him in the basement. If anything, this would avoid one of them getting hurt if she tried moving him herself.

They came up with a game plan for that evening. She would put the dose of sleeping medication in Ben's dinner, and as soon as he went out, Tim would come from outside, where he would be waiting to help get Ben to the basement. Then Tim would leave.

They got up from the table. The plan would be her having dinner ready for five thirty, and that would be the same time Tim showed up and waited outside till she went outside and got him. She was making spaghetti with meatballs because she knew Ben would eat it in seconds without hesitation. She felt bad for betraying her son's trust like this. Even if he was a killer, she still loved him so much, and she wanted him to be good again. It all had to go to plan because if something went wrong, there was no telling what Ben would do.

It was close to five thirty, and dinner had been ready for a while. The anticipation was getting at Amy, and she'd started dinner way too early. She had to stall for a half hour, so she kept busy in the kitchen, making noises like she was still cooking while Ben sat unsuspectingly on the couch watching TV. Five thirty came, and she called Ben in for dinner. He sat down at the table, and as soon as she put the plate in front of him, he dove right in. She couldn't even watch him eat without feeling guilty, so she kept her head down and waited to hear a thud. It followed soon after serving him the meal. She jumped up from her chair to make sure he hadn't choked on any food or fallen in a weird way. She saw he was all right and still breathing, so she lifted him upright and leaned him against the wall. She stood up and quickly walked to the front door. She flung it open, saw Tim standing in the shadows, and waved him in. He slinked across the driveway like he was avoiding being seen. Amy took one last look out the door and closed it behind him as he entered.

They slowly walked into the kitchen, Amy grasping at Tim's arm and on the verge of tears. They stood there staring at Ben, who was sitting against the wall slumped to one side, snoring and drooling. It seemed to make it a lot easier when they saw him as sleeping rather than drugged.

They managed to get him down the steps and to the corner of the basement, where Amy had a chain tied to an existing anchor that was drilled into the wall. She put the chain around his ankle and covered it in a cloth to protect the skin from becoming too irritated. They sat him up against the wall and left a couple of bottles of water beside him for when he got up and Amy wasn't right there. They thought Ben would be out for the rest of the night, but as they were walking up the steps they heard the chain rustle around. When they looked back, Ben was sitting upright in the corner, looking right at them. The way he was sitting and the way the light bounced off his eyes, he looked like a demon sitting in the corner.

Amy and Tim were both stunned. Neither one of them knew what to do or say. A few seconds went by, which for Amy felt like an eternity, and then Ben started nodding off. His chin dropped and then popped back up, as if he was fighting to stay awake. That made his face look even scarier. He would get this mean look on his face and then slowly fade to nothing and nod off again. After about the fourth time of doing this, he succumbed to the drug and went back out. This time he was out for a while.

The next morning, Amy woke up in her bed. She'd barely slept because she'd kept tossing and turning. She couldn't believe she had her son chained up in the basement like an animal.

She pulled herself out of bed and walked over to the basement door. She knew he would be awake, and she would have to face him. She had prepared what she was going to say to him, and she was determined to fix him. She was going to tell him her plan in the hopes that he would cooperate and make things easier rather than a hard struggle. She stood there at the door, playing out every scenario in her head, bad and good. She slowly reached out and grabbed the door knob. As quietly as possible, she turned the knob and pulled the door open. It took her a few seconds to finally take that first step. Step by step, she walked down the stairs as if her calmness would ease some of the anger in Ben. When she took her next step, it would drop her down to where she could see him. That step was the hardest for her to take. She hesitated before she landed on that step, but once she did, she was in complete shock at what she was looking at. It was the only scenario she had not planned for, the one thing she hadn't considered, the only thing that could completely ruin her plan and her life.

Ben was gone!

10
CHAPTER

Amy was staring at an empty chain. She ran down and looked around to see if he was hiding somewhere, but he wasn't. She walked over to the corner she'd had him chained in to try to figure out how he'd escaped. She looked down at the end of the chain where she had it locked around his ankle and noticed the lock wasn't locked anymore. It was as if someone had opened it with a key. She picked it up to inspect it and noticed the tip of a pocketknife broken off in it. Somehow, he'd picked the locked. She regretted not going through his pockets. She knew he carried a little pocketknife with him, but she hadn't thought about it.

None of this sank in until she raced to the top of the steps and into the kitchen but had no idea what to do. She realized she'd messed up big time. There was no telling where he was or whether he was hurting someone else. She had no choice but to call the police.

She ran to the phone, snatched it up, and frantically dialed. It wasn't the police she was calling, though. She had this uncontrollable urge to call Tim and at least warn him that Ben had escaped. She thought that because Ben had seen Tim there, he would want revenge.

Tim agreed that she should call the police, but he came up with the idea of making a missing person claim instead of going completely clean and going to jail. He convinced her that they would pick up Ben and bring him back home.

They talked for a few more minutes, and then she got off the phone and called the police. She gave a description of Ben and told them exactly what he was wearing when he'd left the house.

They took the description and told her to sit tight. They would get in touch when they heard something or found him. They said the best thing to do was stay home in case he came back home, but she knew he wasn't going to do that without a fight. Ben had woken up chained to a wall after being drugged by his own mother. The one person he was supposed to trust.

A few hours went by. Then a few more hours. Before she knew, it was night, and all she had done was sit there staring blankly at the wall. She was jolted back to reality when her silence was interrupted by three loud bangs on the door.

Amy immediately jumped to her feet. Then she froze up, thinking about facing what was on the other side of the door. *Knock, knock, knock.* She jumped again. This time she hurried to the door and flung it open. Standing there was Detective Flex. He had his hand on Ben's shoulder. She looked over at Ben, who was looking down at his feet. He wouldn't look up at her or talk to her. Detective Flex stated that Ben hadn't said a word since he'd been picked up. Flex started asking questions about how things were going and if this was over a fight they were having.

Ben took off into the house. When he did that, Flex tried taking a step into the house, but Amy stepped in front of him, blocking him from coming any farther.

Amy thanked him and hurried him on. Detective Flex had been suspicious of Ben and Amy since day one. He knew there was something that wasn't right with them. He had nothing on them, so he had to respect her wishes. He politely stepped back but gave her some information on seminars and classes for troubled kids, and then went on his way.

She watched him walk down the driveway and closed the door when he got to his car. She slowly turned around, expecting Ben to be standing there with a lot of pent up anger, but he wasn't. He was over on the couch watching TV, completely ignoring her. She stood off to the side, nervously watching him. She didn't know how to react to this, so she decided to talk to him.

She walked over to him and tried making small talk, but all he did was turn up the TV to drown her out. This pissed off Amy, and she turned off the TV at the box. "You have nothing to say? Nothing to ask me?"

Ben shook his head and tried clicking the remote's on button. Amy was standing in front of the sensor, so there was no way he was turning that TV back on.

"Don't you want to know why I chained—"

She was cut off by a correction Ben wanted to make. "Why you *and Tim* chained me!"

"Excuse me?"

"I saw you both walking up the steps last night."

Amy didn't know what to say. She had hoped that he'd forgotten about that, and Tim could stay completely out of it. *Guess that isn't happening now.*

"There's something wrong with you, Ben. You are sick. You like hurting people, and sooner or later that is going to land you in jail, or even worse, dead."

Ben snapped his head toward his mother and without skipping a beat replied, "I don't die, Mom. They do!"

"Who is *they*?"

"Anyone who gets in my way of doing anything!"

Ben jumped up from the couch, went into his room, and closed the door behind him. Amy was left standing in the living room, her mind spinning like a top. She had no idea what to think or how to react to this. Was she now someone he wanted to kill? Was Tim? She knew one thing for sure: she wasn't getting any sleep anytime soon.

She went into the kitchen, the room farthest away from Ben's bedroom, and called Tim in a panic, asking him what to do. Tim, who had not wanted to get involved from the beginning, was reluctant to give any further advice and was vague with his answers. Amy caught on quickly and used it against him. In her old life, she'd picked up some skills that got people to do things they didn't normally. She was a master at manipulation and didn't hesitate to use Tim's love for her against him. By the end of the conversation, Tim was all-in and tried to come up with some solid game plans with her. He also convinced her that Ben had no intentions of hurting her. After all, she was his mother, and there was no love like a son's love for his mother.

Her mind was eased by the time she got off the phone. She felt a lot better, and they both agreed that tomorrow she would try talking to Ben again.

It was getting late, and she had to work in the morning. Before she headed to bed, she went over to Ben's room and quietly opened the door. She tiptoed inside and stood there for a few minutes, admiring her sleeping son. She kissed him on the forehead and then left the room. It took her a little bit before she was able to clear her head and fall asleep.

Later that night she was woken up by a strange feeling. A feeling that someone was watching her. She was too afraid to move or look around for the first few minutes. She hoped it was just in her head but she couldn't shake the feeling someone was in the room with her. She didn't want to give the impression she was awake so she slowly turned her head and looked toward the door. She saw her door was open a crack. There was someone standing there staring at her through the crack of the door. She froze. She couldn't take her eyes off the door and she couldn't close her eyes either. She lay there, not moving a muscle. After a few minutes, the door slowly closed shut and she heard footsteps walking around on the other side.

She was paralyzed with fear. The fight in her wanted to get out of bed and take down whoever that was, even if it was Ben. She'd teach him a lesson. But the flight inside her overwhelmed her, and all she could do was lie there clutching to the blankets, keeping both eyes on the door. She lay there and prayed to God for the first time in a long time. She prayed that her son be delivered back to her from the clutches of evil. She wanted her son back.

It felt like it took a lifetime, but eventually the sun hit her window, and the birds started chirping outside. This was a comforting feeling for her, as if because it was daytime, nothing bad could happen. It gave her the courage to get out of bed and face whatever fear she had of going out there. It was still early in the morning, and she knew Ben would still be sleeping. She thought she had a bit of an advantage by getting up before him—if that was in fact him last night. The first thing she was going to do was see whether the front door was locked. If it was unlocked, she could at least fall asleep another night thinking it was an intruder looking to rob an empty house but left once they saw people were in it.

She got out of bed, opened the door, and stuck her head out to look around. She wanted to make sure the coast was clear before she put herself in a position where she was unable to slam the door shut if something were to come charging out at her.

Ben wasn't up yet, so she walked into the kitchen and put on the coffee. While the coffee was brewing, she walked over to the front door to see if it was locked. She saw that it wasn't locked and almost felt relief. She reached out to lock it and just then, the door swung open. Amy let out a scream and jumped so high and far away that she was almost on the other side of the living room.

Ben walked in, and although he tried not to, he burst into laughter from her reaction. The look on Amy's face, the scream she let out, and how far she'd jumped was hilarious to Ben.

"I'm sorry, Mom. I didn't mean to scare you. I went for a jog this morning," he said through broken laughter.

Amy let out a relieved laugh. "It's okay, sweetie. We needed a good laugh. Want some breakfast?"

Ben was starving and jumped at the opportunity for some breakfast. He had to jump at the opportunity of a shower first, Amy told him. They laughed, and Ben went and had a shower while Amy prepared breakfast.

By the time Ben was out, breakfast was ready and waiting on the table. Ben sat down and was about to dive right in. He had a fork full of delicious scrambled eggs and a big piece of bacon. He put it up to his lips before he suddenly stopped. He pulled the fork away and looked up at Amy. All she could do was apologize and reassure him there was nothing in there that would make him sleepy. It took some convincing, but eventually he trusted her enough and shoveled that big forkful down his gullet.

She saw that as an opening and brought up what had happened the other night. Ben ignored her again and started talking about something else. This was frustrating for Amy, but she didn't want to push it. Things were going good right now, and she didn't want to think about what might happen if she pissed him off more. She still had no way of knowing whether the door was locked, and to avoid raising any questions or suspicion, she didn't want to ask Ben if, when he'd left, the door was locked or unlocked. Even if it was him last night, he could lie and say the door was left completely open, just to mess with her some more. The more she thought about it, the more she stressed. She had a double shift today, and she had to be on her game. There was no way she was going to call April knowing how dangerous Ben really was, but she didn't want to leave him alone either. She didn't know what to do. If she left him alone and he killed someone else, that would be on her. If she called April over to babysit and he killed her, Amy would not be able to live with herself. She decided to go with the lesser evil and leave him alone.

"Ben, can you please stay home today? I have a double, and I don't want to be at work worrying about you."

Ben looked up at her and agreed to stay home. This didn't put Amy's mind at ease. In fact, it made her even more uneasy, thinking he might do something just to spite her.

She had no choice. She had to leave for work or call in sick and not get the pay she needed to make rent. She had no choice. She had to go.

She got to work, and it wasn't very busy at all. She thought maybe calling Ben once an hour to make sure he was at home would help a bit. He answered every time. She first called at eight in the morning, then nine, and then ten. She did this all the way up till eight o'clock that night. When she called that hour, there was no answer. She tried not to panic at first and assumed he must have been in the bathroom or something. She gave it another five minutes and called again. Still no answer. She started to worry a bit. She waited ten minutes and then tried calling again. Nothing. That was when she started to panic. She had two hours left of work, but in the state of mind she was in, the last two hours would feel like an entire shift. Nope, she couldn't do it. She decided to fake an illness and try to ditch out on work. It wasn't busy at all, and there were two other waitresses on shift. She started complaining about stomach pains and was immediately sent home.

On her walk, she thought about what she was going to do if Ben had killed someone else tonight. She power walked home, and by the time she got to her front door, she was out of breath but determined to keep going. She charged in the front door, slammed it shut, and stood silent for a few moments to see if she could hear him.

"Ben!" she yelled.

Out of nowhere, his head popped up for the back of the couch. His tired eyes were barely open. "Mom?" he said with a confused look on his face.

Amy thought it was another one of his tricks and started interrogating him. At first, he answered all her questions and said he had fallen asleep. Amy didn't think it was that simple. She started asking him the same questions but using other words. Ben picked up on it and went to leave the room, but before he left, she made it clear to him that if she called and he was expected to answer, he'd better do so. He smirked and went into his room to go to bed.

It was only ten o'clock at night, and Amy didn't have to be at work the next day until just before the dinner rush. Now that Ben was in his room, she had some time to unwind—something she hadn't done in a very long time. It felt good. She sprawled out on the couch and started channel surfing till she found a movie she liked. She made it about halfway before she fell asleep.

She woke up a couple of hours later to a noise in the kitchen, a loud thud. She sat there silent for a few more seconds to see if she could hear anything. It was quiet. She thought maybe it was her mind playing tricks on her. She turned off the TV, and instead of getting up and walking all the way over to the kitchen, she closed her eyes and went back to sleep.

She woke up once the sun started peeking through the blinds. She tried moving out of the path of the sun but couldn't find a spot to hide her face. She tried turning over, but the sun beating on her back through the window made her start to sweat. She finally sat up, stretched and yawned, and stood up and went into the kitchen to make a pot of coffee, which she felt she desperately needed. She was rubbing her eyes when she walked into the kitchen, so she didn't notice it at first. When she got the coffee going and got her mug ready, she turned around to go to the bathroom before the timer on the pot went off, and she stepped in something wet. She looked down at her feet and jumped back from shock and fear. She wasn't sure exactly what it was, but she stepped in all its blood. She got closer to get a better look and thought it kind of looked like a cat with really big ears. Eventually she determined that it was a rabbit. She instantly assumed it was Ben, and that was that sound she'd heard last night. It was time for her to either accept her role in his life or become the strong hand and take back control.

Just then, Ben came walking out of his room. She thought he looked guilty, but he hid it well. He walked over to where she was and looked down.

"What the fuck is this, Ben?"

Ben looked up at her with a blank, straight face. "How am I supposed to know?"

He started to walk away, which enraged Amy even more. Without thinking, she grabbed Ben by the shoulders, spun him around while kicking his feet out front under him, and landed him right beside the skinned carcass. She got over top of him and brought his face right up to hers. "If you ever bring this shit into my house again, it will be you who will be getting skinned. BY ME!" She threw Ben back to the ground, stood up, walked over to the coffee pot, and poured herself a cup. She turned around and leaned against the counter, stirring her coffee. She looked over at Ben, who was still on the floor and was shocked that his mother had just done that. She hadn't laid a hand on him in a long time. "Now, clean that shit up."

Ben stood up and did exactly what she asked. Then he got cleaned up and came in for breakfast. He sat down at the table but had a completely different demeanor this time. His cocky attitude was gone, and he seemed docile now, like a beaten dog. Amy felt bad, but she'd started fearing for her life, and she needed to do something about it. She was certain now that it was him in her room the other night. Who would stop him from doing it again, or doing something worse next time? She didn't want to take that chance. Maybe now if she could get him to listen to her, she might be able to fix him. *Fix him with discipline*, she thought. It might work. It might make things worse. But she had to try something. She wasn't about to give up.

Things went well after that for about a week. He was listening to her and being kind to people. He was even doing household chores. She thought she was actually getting through. Then one night when she was up late by herself, she went into his room to kiss him on the forehead before she went to bed, and she saw his book sitting on the floor. She saw just the corner of it because it was buried under a bunch of clothes. She quietly snatched it up and left the room. She wanted to take a look inside, and then she was going to put it back. He kept it as a journal and dated every entry. She opened it up to the last entry, and it was dated the fourteenth, which was the day before she'd thrown him on the floor. She thought it was odd he hadn't written in it since then. Maybe it was a sign that he didn't need to express anger like that anymore. She thought it was proof her treatment was working—until she read the entry. It stated very clearly that he wanted to kill Tim and Billy. He had it all plotted out. He was going to make it look accidental, and he had how he was going to do it. He said he would trick Tim into coming in the garage, and he would create a scenario where it looked like Tim had hung himself. For Billy, he thought it would be a good idea to push him in front of a car. There was a steep hill by the one highway that he was going to bring Billy to, and he'd push him down the hill. Billy would roll right into oncoming traffic. It was a very dangerous hill, and there had been a few people who had died that way.

She couldn't believe what she was reading. She'd wanted to believe that because he hadn't done any entries, he was getting better. He didn't need to express his anger the way he was used to. Instead, he'd learned how to get rid of it in other ways. Or so she thought. She'd thought she'd had a good outlet for him, which was showing him yoga and meditation. She now learned it wasn't enough. Monsters were monsters because they had no sympathy or remorse for what they do. She might be able to temporarily change his course, but she'd never change his destination. It was a hard lesson to learn when the monster was someone she loved unconditionally.

11
CHAPTER

Ben woke up shortly after Amy put his book back. He came out, still half asleep and rubbing his eyes, and sat down at the kitchen table across from Amy. "Good morning, Mom," he said through a yawn.

"Good morning, sweetie. How did you sleep?"

"I had a good sleep. Are you hungry?"

"Yeah, I'm just about to start breakfast."

Ben jumped out of his seat. "No, I'll make breakfast this morning!"

Amy sat back down and could hardly contain the big smile it gave her to hear her son say he wanted to cook her breakfast. It's not often he offers to cook, so she was happy to comply. She sat back in her chair, grabbed her coffee and paper, and enjoyed what the daily news had to offer. "I could get used to this," Amy said. She chuckled and poked Ben in the ribs.

Ben let out a laugh and continued focusing on the bacon he was dropping in the hot pan.

Ben behaved like this for a couple of months. He was polite and nonaggressive, turning into a true gentleman. Amy would leave for work, and Ben had no problem staying home by himself. He learned to cook and would even clean the house at night. It was like he was a completely different kid, and Amy loved it. Things were going well. She had stopped bringing Tim around to not set off Ben in any way, but after a while, she started bringing up Tim and Billy in passing. She would say things like, "I was talking to Tim today. They went down to the park and played catch. That sounds like fun, doesn't it?" Ben would usually smile and nod like he didn't really care. Amy didn't know if it was a personal thing from when he saw Tim walking up the steps that one night, or if it was a teenage thing and Ben simply didn't care about anything besides TV and girls.

Either way, it was going on two months, and Ben hadn't had one outburst, one disruptive moment, or any confrontational responses or issues. He had been doing very well, and Amy thought if there was a time to start bringing Tim and Billy back around, it would be now. She knew she needed to be extra cautious.

One night after Amy and Ben finished dinner, they were sitting on the couch when Amy's cell phone rang. It was sitting right beside Ben. He instinctively looked down at the phone and saw Tim's name on it. He didn't give much of a response to it, which Amy thought was a good sign. She picked it up and walked in the other room. A few minutes went by, and she came back and sat back down on the couch. Ben was still sitting there, completely consumed with watching TV, paying no mind to Amy.

"That was Tim. He says hello."

Ben bounced up, "Oh. Tell him and Billy I said hey." Then he went back to watching TV.

Any other person would have noticed the subtle glitches in Ben's personality over the last couple of months. On the surface he seemed like a normal kid, but just under that was a monster trying to break through. The only reason why he hadn't killed anyone was because he knew if he did, it would make it to the news, and that would most definitely put a stop to any plot he had cooking up. Maybe it was Amy's wishful thinking, but anyone could tell that he was biting his tongue and fighting back the urge to hurt people that entire time. The only thing that was holding him back was the thought of revenge. If he had to wear a smile every day to get what he wanted, he would. It would be hard, but he would do it.

Later that night, after Amy made sundaes for dessert, she started talking about Tim and suggested they all go to the park together to play catch. Ben thought it was a great idea, and that next weekend they threw the ball around in the park with Tim and Billy. Ben was running around with Billy and treating him like a brother, showing Billy how to catch or throw the ball. He would lead him around and show him stuff. Ben also treated Tim like a father figure, asking Tim questions only a son would ask a dad.

They spent a while there, hanging out. There was one point that made Amy feel uneasy. She and Tim were sitting at the picnic tables when she looked over and saw Ben standing beside Billy at the river. Ben had his hand on Billy's arm, and they were both leaning in toward the water and looking at something Ben was pointing at. To anyone else, it looked like two kids standing by a river, and it looked like Ben had Billy by the arm to keep him from falling in. But not to Amy. She saw it as a potential disaster. She instantly got up, walked over there, and nonchalantly joined in. She played it off as if she was coming there to tell them it was time to leave. They loaded up and got in the car. Tim was skeptical coming back around after all the stuff Amy told him, but he wasn't the kind of guy that had women throwing themselves at him and he made his decision to stick around based on loneliness and a need for love, rather than the facts and dangers that were presented. Tim even started to believe that Ben was getting better. He thought if he kept a close eye on the situation, he could control it and help this damaged family become normal again.

Tim and Billy started coming around a lot more, and Ben played the part. He would pretend to love having them there until he found his opportunity to make his move. Ben had it all planned out regarding what he was going to do. He even had it written down in detail in the book Amy had found. But she'd been blinded by manipulation and optimism. Ben was good at getting people to think how he wanted them to think, and he used it to his advantage.

It was Saturday morning, and Amy was waking up to get ready for her double shift. She was trying to be quiet so as to not wake Tim, who was sleeping next to her. Tim was a light sleeper and instantly woke up the moment she pulled herself out of bed. Even first thing in the morning, Amy looked beautiful in her long white T-shirt. She walked around to Tim's side of the bed and sat down on the edge of the mattress. She leaned down, gave him a kiss on the forehead, and then went to get back up.

Tim pulled her back down, wrapping her in his arms. "Nope, you're not allowed to leave my arms ever again."

Amy giggled and lay there for a moment. She thought about her last relationship and then about this relationship. She couldn't help but feel so lucky to have such a great guy after such a shitty past. She hugged him tight and whispered, "I love you," in his ear. Then she got up and started getting ready for work.

Tim suggested that he stay with Ben today since Billy was at a friend's place for a sleepover all weekend. Amy loved the idea of them hanging out together alone all day, but she also had that voice in the back of her head saying it was a bad idea. She had this gut feeling that Ben was still a monster, but she ignored it and thought it was paranoia. When Tim suggested spending the day with Ben, that paranoia hit her hard. She tried suggesting he do something else in a way that wouldn't gain suspicion, but he insisted he stay. She pushed that gut feeling down and went to work. She knew it was going to be a busy day, and she had to focus on work and not worry about what was happening back home. She voiced her concern, but he still suggested he stay. "What could he possibly do to me? He's a kid, and I'll be paying attention." Tim's confidence made Amy feel a bit better his unconditional love for her made him want to risk it all and help her. There was a good chance that she wouldn't be able to come home during the break between shifts, so she kissed Tim goodbye before she left, sneaked into Ben's room and kissed him goodbye, and then headed out the door for work.

A couple of hours later, Tim woke up to the sound of the TV turning on. He looked at the clock: it was just after nine. *Time to get out of bed,* he thought.

When he walked out of the bedroom, he saw the coffee machine was running. Ben looked over. "Good morning. I made you some coffee."

Thankful for the gesture, Tim walked over to the pot and poured himself a cup without thinking twice. He put his cream and sugar in it and sat down beside Ben. "What do you want to do today?" Tim asked.

"I'm not really feeling well. I kind of want to just stay home today, if that's okay with you."

It was haunting how innocent and fake someone could be. Ben didn't even try to hide the fact that he wasn't actually feeling sick at all. This should have raised a few red flags, but Tim thought he was being a normal, lazy kid who just wanted to watch TV. Tim went with it and agreed to hanging out at home. Tim made some breakfast for the two of them, and they sat there watching TV for the better part of the day.

Amy called on her break between shifts and said it was so busy that she didn't have time to even go to the bathroom during her shift. One of the girls had called in sick, and they couldn't find anyone to replace her. That meant it was just the two servers on the floor.

Tim reassured her everything was going well, and he and Ben were both about to start prepping for dinner. They were going to make tacos together and then watch a few movies afterward. This put Amy's mind at ease, and before she knew it, it was time to go back to work. They got off the phone with each other, and then Tim started getting everything ready for dinner. Tim was more focused on getting dinner ready while Ben made cinnamon rolls for dessert.

Tim couldn't believe how well they were getting along. They did do a lot of watching TV, but they also talked, and Ben ended up opening up to Tim a bit. That was something Tim hadn't expected. Ben showed a very vulnerable side of himself that he had never exposed before in front of Tim.

Tim didn't realize it, but all Ben was doing was gaining Tim's trust to use it against him another time.

They finally finished cooking dinner and sat down to eat. By the time they left the table, they had eaten almost everything they had made. There was some stuff left over for Amy for when she got home from work.

After they were done eating, Ben got up and started clearing the table. Tim helped, and they cleaned everything up and did the dishes together. Tim smoked, so when they were done with the dishes, Tim headed outside to have a cigarette before dessert. Tim got outside and was about halfway done with his smoke when Ben came walking outside with two cinnamon rolls in his hand. It was a nice night out, so they decided to hang out outside for a bit while they ate their dessert. Ben was only done with a quarter of his before Tim had completely devoured his. As Tim took his last bite, Ben told Tim about a project he was working on in the shed out back, and he wanted to show Tim. They walked out back, and Ben opened the door and led the way inside. It was completely dark in there because Ben hadn't yet turned on the light. While Tim stood there waiting for the lights to come on, he started feeling dizzy. He lost his footing and fell to the floor. He leaned against the wall, trying to not lose consciousness, when the lights turned on. Tim could still see a bit, although everything was blurry. Before he went completely out, he saw a rope hanging from the roof and a milk crate underneath it. The other side of the rope was very long and swung around a few more poles, like a pulley system. Tim tried with all his might to get back up. With every piece of strength and fight he had left, he managed to make it to his knees. He went to get up on both feet so he could at least stumble toward the door, and scream for help before he went out completely, but once he tried to get from his feet, Ben came up from the side and very easily pushed him back down to the ground.

That was it for Tim. There was nothing left inside of him. He fought for a few more seconds to keep his eyes open, but everything went from blurry to black.

Tim woke up a little while later. He was sitting upright on a chair. His wrists were bound together with a T-shirt and then wrapped with duct tape to show no evidence of being tied up. When Tim came to, he was really groggy and still a bit out of it.

Tim had wanted to connect with Ben so badly that he couldn't see the manipulation happening right under his nose, and before he realized it, it was too late. He started to panic. He kept whipping his head around, trying to see where Ben was. He couldn't see him anywhere. He tried to struggle his way out. Wiggling his wrists back and forth trying to free them.

He felt an aggressive tug on the rope, almost lifting him right off the seat. He started choking, but his mouth was taped shut in the same fashion as his wrists were, so it was difficult and painful when he started coughing through his nose.

Ben walked to where Tim could see him and stood there with a big grin on his face, holding the other end of the rope that went through a series of pulleys to make lifting deadweight easier.

Right before Ben yanked down on the rope, his face went from a creepy grin to an evil stare. With three slow, short pulls on the rope, Tim was hoisted in the air, where he struggled and kicked till there was no life left in him. Ben waited a few minutes before he undid all the tape and took off the T-shirts wrapped around Tim's mouth and wrists. He inspected the body to make sure there was no evidence of him being bound, and he cleaned up everything he had set up.

Ben stood there and admired the lifeless body swinging in the dim light that lit the shed. He observed the body sway back and forth, back and forth. He watched this scene for a half an hour before he disappeared from the scene without a trace.

Later that night, when Amy got home, Ben was already in bed, sleeping. She didn't see Tim anywhere, but his truck was still out front. She thought maybe he'd gone for a walk and would be back soon. She got undressed and showered after a long day of work. Days like that was what made coming home to a clean house with a loving family worth every second of the hardship she endured at work. Being on her feet all day was a killer, but she was starting to see its worth for once in her life.

An hour went by, and she still hadn't heard anything from Tim. She was starting to worry, so she woke up Ben to ask where he had gone. Ben said he'd gone for a walk right after dinner and never come back.

Amy tried calling his house all night. She went walking around the block to see if he had fallen and hurt himself. She walked all over town, but still nothing.

It was about four in the morning when Amy came back from her second lap around the town. She didn't have any luck that time either. She dragged her feet and hung her head as she headed up the driveway. She got to the front door and reached out to grab the knob when something caught her attention out of the corner of the eye. It was like a flicker, or a very quick movement, but whatever it was, it drew her attention to the shed out back. She looked at it, and for some reason it felt like it was looking back at her. Like it knew where Tim was.

Her hand dropped back down to her side. She turned toward the shed and slowly started walking up to it. She'd never noticed how creepy the shed looked in the dark, until tonight.

As she walked up, her footsteps got slower and slower. That gut feeling came back, and this time she couldn't push it out of the way. As she reached out for the handle on the door, she started getting butterflies, and not the good kind. They were the kind that made her want to lose her dinner.

She pressed down on the handle and unlatched the door, which slowly opened. It was very dark and very quiet, except for a creaking sound. She couldn't figure out what the sound was, and then she saw the light fixture slightly swinging back and forth. *Maybe it's the draft moving it,* she thought. But if she listened closely, she would have noticed that the sway of the light didn't sync with the sound.

She reached over to the wall and felt for the light switch. Her fingers finally met the switch, and she flicked on the lights.

She let out a loud scream and then ran back inside and dialed 911.

"What is your emergency?"

"I just found my boyfriend handing from a rope in the garage!"

"Do you know what happened?"

"No. I came home from work, and he was hanging in the garage. Please send someone."

Amy was hysterical and kept having to repeat everything twice from sobbing so hard. She also didn't want to wake up Ben. She wanted to turn him into the police, and she didn't want him waking up before they got there. She was finally able to spit out the address in a manner the operator could understand, and the police were sent over right away.

When the police arrived, Amy was sitting out on the front steps waiting. They pulled up with their lights off, so they didn't disturb the neighbors. It was Detective Flex and Detective Coal.

"This isn't a coincidence, is it?" Amy asked as the detectives walked up the driveway.

"No, ma'am. Any call from dispatch that relates to this address is directly sent to my phone. Now, what's going on here, Ms. Willis?"

Amy grabbed the railing and pulled herself up from the steps. "How about I just show you?"

As they walked back to the shed, she explained to them what had happened and how she'd found him. Detective Flex scanned the property. When he looked over at the house, he locked eyes on Ben, who was standing in the window watching.

At first it seemed innocent enough, but after a moment Detective Flex saw something dark. It unsettled him enough that in those few moments, he convinced himself that Ben was connected to everything weird that had been happening.

Ben turned around and moved out of sight, and Detective Flex walked into the shed.

At first glance, it looked like an obvious suicide. Detective Coal instantly called it out.

Detective Flex, on the other hand, started examining the body even closer. He looked at the wrists and ankles to see if there were any restraint marks. He looked in his mouth to see if there were abrasions from something being stuffed in there. He looked at the fingernails to see if there was any skin wedged between the nail and skin. All came up negative.

Amy stood off to the side while they looked over the scene. She was biting her nails so hard that they made a loud popping sound. It was so loud that Detective Coal asked her to stop because it was breaking his concentration. The more they looked around, the more they realized there was nothing to indicate anything other than a suicide.

They tried explaining this to Amy. She finally broke down and told Detective Flex everything—except her murdering her husband. She said it with such fear that they believed her.

She told them about Mr. Anderson. She told them about David and the old man. She told them about the old lady and how Ben had shoved her into the mixer. But none of this meant anything without evidence. There was nothing they could do. The only thing they offered was to keep a close watch on him. They also offered to bring him downtown to scare him and see if they could get him to confess about something, but they came to the conclusion that if he didn't break, it would make it so much worse for Amy at home.

The first thing they had to do was clean up the mess at hand. Then they would come up with a game plan to build evidence against Ben.

For the next twenty-four hours, their house was nothing but police tape and flashing lights. Amy couldn't wait till it was all over. She wanted everyone gone. She needed to grieve in peace. She loved this man, and she'd found him hanging. She was devastated.

Ben loved it. He loved the film crew being out front, he loved all the cops being there, and he especially loved the fact that he'd gotten away with it—and it was right in his backyard!

It was Sunday night, and the phone started ringing. Amy was slow to get up from the couch but finally reached the phone before the answering machine picked it up. It was Billy. He was ready to be picked up from his sleepover. Amy's heart sank in her stomach. She was able to get out, "Hey, buddy."

"Hey, Amy. I can't get hold of Dad. Is he there? I'm ready to come home."

Amy didn't know what to do, but she knew she couldn't tell him the truth over the phone. "I haven't talked to him all day. His truck is here, but he isn't," Amy said.

"Well, could you come pick me up?" Billy asked.

"Of course. Put your friend's mom on the phone so I can get directions."

Amy had to tell the friend's mother what was going on, and she asked if she knew of any family in the area she could call. She had no luck.

Amy had no idea what to do at this point. She feared for Billy's life, but she had no choice but to bring him back home, call the police and have them look for one of his family members in the area. She got the directions, picked up Billy, and brought him back home. She did her best not to let on that anything was wrong, and she got Billy tucked into her bed without one outburst.

Once she got back into the living room, her thoughts on her monster son, her dead boyfriend, and now her dead boyfriend's son consumed her mind. She called the police and asked if they could look into finding another family member, to which they complied, but there was no place for him to go until they found someone in the family and the police suggested he stay there with Amy till they could locate a family member. She didn't want to say no and raise suspicion and try to make up a lie as to why he couldn't stay there. She was caught between an innocent life and her son's life. She lay on the couch as her mind raced. It was all her fault, and if she had been a better mother, none of this would have happened.

She didn't get any sleep that night. Billy and Ben woke up at around the same time. Amy was in the kitchen pouring coffee when Ben walked in. "Good morning, Mom," he said with a big grin.

Amy didn't say anything at all. Billy came walking out a few minutes later, rubbing his eyes. "Good morning, guys. Have you heard anything from my dad?"

Ben perked up. It was like he wanted to hear her tell Billy his dad was dead.

Amy looked over at Billy, who was sitting there eating cereal. "Do you have any grandparents that live around here? Or any aunts and uncles?"

Billy looked up from his big bowl of cereal. "I don't know any of my family. My mom died a long time ago, and I have never met my dad's family."

Amy didn't know what to say. She had to get up and leave before she started crying in front of them. She ran into her room and cried so hard into her pillow that by the time she was done, her pillow was completely soaked.

She lay in her bed for a bit, listening to them in the living room. They were watching a movie. All she wanted to do was hear back from Detective Flex as soon as possible. She didn't know how long she could pretend to love this monster anymore. She wanted it to be over. She wanted him to get real help, and she wanted to figure out what to do with Billy. If anything, the detectives would be able to find someone.

All this stuff raced through Amy's brain as she lay there and listened to the TV. Then she noticed that, other than the TV, it was very quiet. Her head instantly cleared, and the fact that she'd left Billy alone with Ben came rushing into her head like a freight train. She jumped out of bed faster than a bullet and swung open the door. Her worst fear was realized. There was nobody there, and their shoes and coats were gone.

She ran out the front door to see whether they were at least on the property. She ran to the end of the driveway and looked down the road but couldn't see them. She ran to the backyard to see whether they were back there. Nothing. She started to panic. It felt like everything was collapsing on her at once. She started hyperventilating, and everything started to go white. She fell to her knees and let out a deep cry before she folded over and rolled onto her back. As she lay there, staring up at the blue sky and thinking about how fucked up her life was, she was able to pull out one tiny memory that was sitting there, a memory that gave her enough motivation to get up and go find Billy. She thought it was a long shot, but she'd gone through Ben's book. There was a steep hill that had a highway at the bottom of it. She knew where it was and thought there was a good chance they would be there.

She ran back into the house, grabbed the keys, and jumped in the truck. She made it to the bridge in just a few minutes, and she saw Ben and Billy hanging around the edge of the bridge.

Ben started coaxing Billy over to the side, where he was going to shove him off the hill before he spotted Amy. Billy didn't notice her.

It was a windy day and yelling at the top of her lungs didn't seem to catch Billy's attention, so Amy ran. She ran as fast as she could. She ran up the hill where Billy and Ben came into plain view. Ben had Billy standing right on the edge of the hill and was seconds away from pushing him over. Amy ran even harder. At the same time Ben pushed Billy, she leaped into the air, knocking Ben off to the side in the process. She was able to grab Billy and keep him from falling, but with the way she was positioned, there was no way she could pull herself up.

Ben got to his feet and walked over to Amy, who was still struggling to hold on to Billy. "Why are you here?" he shouted at Amy as he knelt beside her. "You were not supposed to be here. You were not supposed to put me in this position."

Amy could barely hang on, and her face was in the dirt. The only thing that was keeping her from letting go was her having her foot hooked around a rock that was sticking out of the ground. "Please, Ben. Help us."

"I'm sorry, Mom. You did this. Not me." Ben stood up and scanned the hills and scenery. "I guess this is as good a place to die as any." He chuckled, leaned down, and kissed his mother on the forehead. "I guess every bird has to leave the nest at some point."

Amy lay there, knowing exactly what Ben's intentions were.

Ben stood up, slowly walked around to the back of his mom where her foot was hooked into the rock and gave it a light tap with his foot. It was all that was needed for Amy's strength to give way and let go completely. Once she did, she was propelled down the hill as if someone had tied a rope to both of them and yanked on it.

Billy didn't stand a chance of catching himself. He hit every rock on the way down and was barely alive by the time he hit the road. Amy was able to get upright because she was sliding down on her butt, and once she did that, she was able to somewhat control her speed. Ben watched nervously as she started to slow down to almost a complete stop. But just before she came to a halt, her heel was jammed up on a rock sticking a few inches out of the ground, which sent her flying forward. There was no recovery from that. She came down on her face with such a hard crash that it knocked her out. Billy hit the pavement first, and as luck would have it for Ben, a transport truck came by and ran him over. Amy went flying down the hill, and by the time she made it to the bottom, she slammed into the side of the transport truck and was instantly sucked under the wheels. The truck came to a screeching halt, and all that was left behind the truck was a trail of blood and body parts—and Ben standing at the top of the hill, looking down.

The truck driver ran to the back of the truck, his hands on his head in disbelief. He scanned the scene and tried to figure out what had happened. Then he looked up and saw Ben standing there, emotionless, observing.

The trucker ran back to the cab and dispatched for help.

It was only a few minutes before the area was swarming with cops, and they shut down the highway. Ben stood there and watched from the same spot. All the cops were down at the scene—except one. Ben felt the presence of someone walking up behind him, and he had a pretty good idea of who it was. The footsteps got closer and closer till they came to a stop a few feet beside Ben.

"What did you do?" Detective Flex calmly asked.

Ben shifted to his side so that he faced the detective. "What do you mean?"

"Is that how you want to play it, Ben?"

Ben didn't answer. He simply turned back toward the highway.

"You know, if you confess to me right now, the law will go easy on you. If you lie, and we find out you have been lying, I will personally make sure you never see the light of day again. So having said that, is there anything you want to tell me about what happened here today?"

Ben looked up at the detective and then back down at the crime scene. "I am not really sure what happened. I was standing over there." He pointed to where Detective Coal was standing a few meters back. "I heard my mom scream, and by the time I looked back, she and Billy were gone. That's when I walked over to the ledge and saw that they'd fallen."

Detective Flex flipped his notepad closed. "So that's it, then? You have nothing else you want to say to me?"

"Yes, actually," Ben replied. "Can I get a ride home?" Without even waiting for a response, Ben walked toward the detective's car and jumped in the back seat.

Detective Flex walked over to where Detective Coal was standing.

"What's going to happen to him?" Coal asked.

"Foster system, probably." Flex shoved his shades up on his nose and then walked over to the car.

"You know, we could just toss his ass down the hill, call it another suicide," Coal said over the roof of the car before getting in.

Flex looked over at his partner before getting into the car. "One day, we will regret not doing exactly that."